My Saintly Demon

Contents

Author's Note

While I rarely write anything that needs content warnings, I feel you need to be aware of a few things before reading.

This book contains strong anti-Catholic sentiments and may be offensive to some. There is also on page drug and alcohol abuse.

Should any of these things cause you distress, please do not continue reading.

CHARLES

I'm a man living a terrible lie.

Preaching about the evils of sin while overindulging in every single one I can.

Gluttony? Check.

Sloth? I'm a fucking master.

Lust? Well, that's the one that brought me to my knees. Literally and figuratively.

Raising the tiny disc of unleavened bread over my head, I repeat the same damn prayer every time I bless the symbolic white wafer. Every time I mutter the blessed words under my breath and the altar boy rings his bell, I die a little inside.

Being the shining example for a community, when sainthood couldn't be farther from the truth, is hard. If they knew what I keep hidden in the back of my closet and buried in the depths of my mind, all the adoring looks would be in the past. The pious pearl-clutchers in front of me would banish me as far as they could.

Shunned by the very flock I've shaped and built for the last ten years of my life.

Breaking the wafer, I place the dry, tasteless morsel on my tongue and wash it down with bitter wine. Just like I do every mass. It balls in my stomach like poison. I want to vomit with the hundreds of pairs of eyes trained on me. Regarding me like I'm something so special. Something to be revered. But I'm not.

Not anymore.

Maybe I once was, but I too have found a light to follow. It's probably darker and not very helpful to most of the people shuffling to the front of the church, but it's what I need to find my way.

Taking my place at the front of the altar, I distribute the sacrament of communion like the most precious gift to the people of my parish. There's a reason they refer to members of a parish as a flock. Sheep follow commands without question. Led from place to place with no thought of their own.

I've done this. Led them down this righteous and holy path. For what? A false sense of security that they're doing the right thing? That the church's way is the only way? I wonder how many would still talk to me if they knew what I've been up to?

Mass ends and I paste the fake smile and pious attitude on, along with the fancy robe I wear, and mingle with my *flock*. It's gotten harder to do this with each passing day. My stomach grows more sour with every extra second of the charade.

I fucking hate this farce I've become.

"Great sermon, Father."

"Father, I was so touched by your homily."

"Father, I'm so happy to hear your message of truth today."

I tune them all out and nod with a hollow thanks or, if I'm feeling extra wordy, *glad to hear it*. I hate this part about mass because sometimes they want to talk and I don't. I hate faking every single thing in my life from sunrise to sunset.

When the last congregation member has thankfully left, I do my final walk around. Checking locks and turning off lights as my shined-up shoes click over the tiles and slide over carpets. Collecting the silk scarf Mrs.Watson has left behind again. Stupid woman. I've stopped leaving a note with it in the lost and found. She knows it's here. I'm positive she leaves it on purpose hoping for me to invite her over to pick it up. If only she knew my temptation could never be the fault of a woman.

I need a damn drink. It's the only way I can cope with life these days. Alcohol and marijuana numb my existence. This shallow bubble of a life, with no more depth than a shadow puppet on the bedroom door, seems less bleak in a gin soaked haze.

Finally, in the rectory's safety, I lock the door behind me before stripping off my clothes, tossing my collar with no care onto the coffee table as I pass by it. Leaving my clothes in a heap in the hallway, I step into the shower.

The hot water turns my skin pink as I lean my head against the tiles and release the dam of tears I've barely kept at bay. When the water turns cold, I finally step out and wrap a fluffy towel around myself before walking to the kitchen for a gin and tonic, double.

I down the first one with ease and mix another. Adding a splash of lime this time. Alcohol doesn't solve the problem, but it sure makes it go away for a while. Not long enough, but I'll take the temporary escape for now as I contemplate the shitshow of my life.

Not caring about any kind of decorum in this church paid for abode I have to live in, I let the towel drop to the floor and my bare ass hit the upholstery of the hideous lime green suede couch. Who knew the 70s would make a comeback in style and the parish would spend a crapload of money decorating a house I live in without my input?

Ha! Silly question. Of course, they don't care about me or what I think. That's obvious in how they're taking the Bishop's side. I'm just a parish priest. I'm disposable.

The second drink goes down quickly and calls for a third. The happy buzz of alcohol already floats through my brain. Naked and giggling, I pad back to the kitchen and instead of mixing another drink; I tuck the bottle of gin under my arm, grab a few cans of tonic water from the fridge and carry them to the living room with me. No sense getting up every time. I can get shit-faced faster if I limit the amount of distractions and movements.

There's no better time than when you're drunk to face the music of your impending job loss, though, is there? Not that I'm sad to leave this pit of fake leather and smiles, but I want to leave on my own terms and it's not going as planned.

Nothing in my life is going as planned.

I'm supposed to be preaching to these people to love one another and be kind, and we are all cut from the same cloth, yet behind closed doors it's a different story.

Much different.

The final straw was not helping the young gay man struggling with his family's decision to turn him away and facing the same addictions I was. His wealthy family is a major contributor to the church and we shouldn't make them angry. We don't want them to pull their donations after all.

Instead, I'm repeatedly asked to ignore someone's plea for help.

From a man who's so much like me, I might as well be looking in a mirror.

The gin bottle is a quarter empty and my anger bubbles to the top as I finally read over the stack of paper left in my mailbox. The sterile font and type does nothing to simmer my ire, as I read the words sent to me from someone who promised never to reveal my secrets or leave me.

The only man I ever loved. Bishop Matthew. My boss.

> *Charles,*
>
> *I hope this letter finds you well. As you can see, our lawyers have suggested the following course of action and I agree with the diocese to terminate your residency here.*
>
> *We will pay you a handsome severance with the understanding you will remain silent and follow the gag order we propose.*

> *Please respond by the due date so we may solve this matter post haste.*
>
> *Regards,*
>
> *Bishop Matthew*

"Regards, Bishop Matthew," I slur in the snottiest voice I can muster. "You can kiss my ass. Actually, you *have*. I'm not hiding anymore. Take your severance and fuck off, you poor excuse for a human being."

Tossing the paper on the coffee table, my hands shaking, I don't understand how words can hurt so much. It wasn't supposed to be like this. Now it's my mess to deal with.

Alone.

My head spins with rage and alcohol, but mostly for the request that I hide myself indefinitely. I'm done with all the goddamn secrets and lies.

I'm done faking my way through my job and life.

I won't do it.

Pouring myself another drink, probably not the best idea, I fumble around on my laptop and find my favourite porn site. Today I want to watch all the bodies. All the dicks. The filthier the better. I'm in that kind of mood.

The site loads and I choose the first video offered from the list. Four men taking turns with each other, sucking cocks, fucking and coming all over each other. The scene is the perfect distraction, and yet, it also reminds me of what I've missed. Sure, it's pure animal behaviour and sex purely for physical gratification, but it's more than that to me.

They get to express themselves openly. They can have other men touch them. People are watching. Well, not the public, but they're in a group and obviously happy to be there. Base behaviour is still something new to me. Years of suppressing myself and what I want have come to a breaking point. Rather than try to sop up the mess, I let the rage boil over.

Matthew opened my eyes to what I'd so desperately stuffed aside. I wanted another person to love me in a physical way. They didn't even need to love me romantically. I'd be a booty call, if that's all I get. To be fair, I think that's how it all started. Just us finally seeking that forbidden human intimacy. Finding our way through the sneaking around and hiding was at first a thrill, but as the novelty of it wore off, I noticed what it really was.

We broke our vows to the church, but even worse, in their eyes, it was with a person of the same sex. Nothing good would come from it, but I kept on doing it. When I let my emotions get involved with Matthew, it changed everything. It scared me to death when I realized I loved him. That was a love I'd had to work hard at hiding. Hiding being gay was one thing, but hiding how I felt for a person I loved having naked against me, someone whose lips so intimately kissed mine, was quite another. Sins of the flesh are far less confusing when there are no emotions involved.

Matthew sensed it. He knew I was in deep and he was at risk of being outed because of it. He tried to make me believe this was for the best and he'd find me again in a few years. You know, when it's safe. Like a few years of waiting would solve all the problems of the Catholic church. But love or not, this new freedom to be who I wanted was the driving force behind this shit-storm.

If only I hadn't drunk so much I could get my dick on board with the video and enjoy it more. I could take my mind off things. It twitches half-heartedly as I tug on my balls, but it's not happening tonight. And yet I can't turn the scene off or look away.

Not until the video ends and instead of fading to a black screen or rolling credits, two of the men share a tender kiss as the other wipes the mess off his chest. It's the look in the man's eyes as he gazes at the other two that has me slamming my laptop closed harder than I should.

Naked, in the darkening room, I say to hell with the tonic water and drink the gin straight from the bottle.

Dave

"Dave! Get the fuck over here!"

I rise from the bar stool, buttoning my suit jacket as I walk to the back room my father summoned me to. Because that's what it is, summoning the demon spawn to be yelled at. I should be used to it by now.

My father, one of Satan's right-hand men twice removed, swirls his glass of whiskey as he leans forward on the black leather couch. A glance around the room reveals my two older brothers present, and I quickly dampen the flames of a fight in my eyes. If they're both here, this doesn't bode well for me.

"Sit down, Dave. We need to talk."

My father's voice rumbles and carries the authoritative tone you don't ignore if you want to remain standing. My brothers both stand at attention in their custom-made suits. Their expressions remain blank as they follow my walk across the room to our father.

Wiping my sweaty hands on my pants, I perch on the edge of the leather sofa across from him. It's the finest Italian leather you could ever want for a piece of furniture. Rumour has it our father made a tempting bargain with an upscale furniture designer. We never lack in the finer things. Pure decadence, just like the whiskey he has in his glass. Fifty-year-old Glen Livet at twenty-five thousand dollars a bottle. There are some perks to hell.

"Sure, what's this about?" My back is straight as I drum my fingers on my knee. A nervous habit that my father picks up on.

"You're nervous Dave. Do you know why?"

"No, sir."

The ice clicks in his glass as he takes a sip, watching me over the rim with his cold, blue eyes.

"What do you think a demon should be like, Dave? Are there any defining attributes?"

"You've always taught us we should revel in the debauchery of all kinds and take no shame in it."

He nods, a small grin in place. "But what else, son? Surely there's more to it than that?"

I swallow. Of course there is, and it's the part I always struggle with.

"Demons shouldn't show mercy, and we are here to raise hell for mortals."

The ice clinks in his glass again and my brothers' gazes burn into me. Flames of anger rise behind my eyes with their silent judgment, but I stamp the heat out immediately. If I show anger towards my father or brothers right now, I'll be leaving this room in a dustpan.

"Dave, I asked you to pay a visit to the gentleman who was making TikTok videos denouncing Satan and selling vials of anti-demon potion, whatever the fuck that is. Did you do it?"

I swallow. "I did."

"Hmmm... what was the outcome?"

"He promised he'd stop."

My brother grunts and I shoot a look in his direction. He shakes his head and a smile plays on his lips.

"Dave, I gave you direct orders, and you didn't follow them. That makes me look bad." He drains his whiskey, reaches for a coaster and places his empty glass on it. It's a teak table. One needs to be careful about water stains. "I don't like to look bad."

Reclining, he throws an arm across the back of the sofa. Those icy blue eyes continue to bore into me.

"I'm sorry."

My other brother barks out a laugh and quickly schools his expression when my father aims a stare in his direction.

"That's your problem, Dave. Demons are never sorry. You should never apologize. *Never.* Yet you constantly do. It's like you're a misplaced Canadian tourist or something, always saying sorry for the littlest things."

"Sorry."

I cringe when the flames flicker behind his cold blue eyes. I can't help it. I mean, you can be a dick and still apologize after. I'm a demon, not a thoughtless monster.

"Unacceptable, Dave. Why the hell did you not take that guy

out as I asked? You have one chance to give me your reason. Make it good."

"I was going to, I was. But when I got to his place, he had this really cool set-up outside for his pet rabbit. You should have seen it. It was genius, and the bunny was just so cute! Like, he was super fluffy, and had the biggest ears, and when he yawned he —"

"Dave!"

This is it. I'm about to die.

"I just couldn't do it because who would take care of the bunny if his owner disappeared? It didn't feel right."

My father rubs the bridge of his nose with a long-suffering sigh and closes his eyes. "You wanted to save the rabbit, so you didn't kill the man?"

"Yes."

"And what kind of promise did you have him make for me to believe he's going to stop making his anti-demon videos?"

When I don't answer immediately, his eyes blink open and he returns his gaze to me.

"I'm waiting."

"I told him if he sent me pics every day of his bunny, I'd spare his life."

"You've got to be fucking kidding me."

"Not even a little bit. Have you ever seen a rabbit yawn, father? It's the cutest thing."

"Jesus fucking christ. This is worse than I thought." He stands, hands in his pockets and stares down at me. Flames flicker behind his eyes and the heat rolls off him in giant waves. He's mad, but not fireball mad. "I'm sending you to earth for a week. You won't be able to come home until I say so, and that's *if* I say so. If you can't figure out how to stop apologizing and making deals involving rabbit photos instead of souls, you're going to stay there."

"A week!? But how will I survive and stay hidden for that long? I can't do that!"

It's one thing to not obliterate a guy for spewing demon hate on the internet, but it's quite another to have to stay on earth for a week and deal with humans twenty-four-seven. Even if they have cute bunnies, they're incredibly complex creatures to me. I've never been there longer than twenty-four hours before. It's like throwing me in the deep end when I can't swim.

The knowing gaze on my father's face tells me that's exactly the point of all this. I need to be less apologetic, more demon-like. I need to stop showing mercy and take what I want because I can. If I can't do that, I won't be welcome back here.

"When you walk through that door, you'll be in the worst place a demon can find himself. Figure out how to survive it and you can come back. If you can't..."

I stand up, straightening my suit again and exit the room with no more words. As I pass by the chair I was in earlier, I tuck my demon handbook in my coat pocket. If I'm going to be on an extended visit, I'm going to need some guidance.

There are a lot of things I've not done well as a demon. I know I'm too nice. But being with humans is going to take some time to figure out. I don't know if I can do it in a week.

With a final breath, I open the door and step into my punishment.

Hell on earth.

CHARLES

Go ahead and add performing a funeral mass with a raging hangover to my list of transgressions.

I'm not even sorry about it. Well, I'm sorry someone lost a person they loved, but I'm not sorry I wasn't responsible enough to remain sober to come to work. And no, I don't want to hear about how it's an unhealthy coping mechanism. I know it's not. But right now, it's the only thing that works.

Once I've spoken to the bishop and told him to go fuck himself, preferably with the horse-sized dildo in his dresser drawer and not enough lube, I should be able to move on and put this shit show behind me. Although, we need to have words over this gag order bullshit. I'm so tired of being the one dumped on. The one everyone just assumes will do as told because I always have.

Making sure I lock the rectory behind me, I immediately go to my closet and behind all the clothes I never seem to wear since I'm always in this goddamn robe, I find the old cookie tin hidden behind my favourite Doc Martens from high school and flip open the lid. Bills of all kinds spill out when the lid pops off. Twenties and fifties and ten dollar bills burst out. I've skimmed from the offering plate for so long now, I'm on my fourth cookie tin. Every time it gets full, I drive three towns over and deposit the cash into a bank account not connected to my working life. The parish knows where I bank and it wouldn't shock me if they know my bank balances. Last time I checked, I had over ten thousand dollars in my secret account. Not a fortune by any means, but it will buy me some time while I figure out what to do with my life. While the letter promises me a large amount of hush money, I'm skeptical they will follow it through.

I've been double-crossed already, after all.

Stuffing the money I skimmed earlier into my stash, I shed my clothes as I walk back to the living room. When I became a priest, not once did I ever think such a dark side would bubble out of me.

Stealing from the offering plate? Drunk on the job? Sex with the bishop?

I never thought that was who I was. But somehow it feels right. When the bishop ended our affair, I threw off the rose-coloured glasses of living life chained to a church. It was more than a simple affair to me. I sacrificed not only my reputation, but my sanity. Matthew's rejection sent me in a rapid downward spiral. While I should be worried about what comes next, I'm not giving it headspace.

I'm going to enjoy the baser things in life and not feel a damn bit guilty doing it.

Digging out the lighter and marijuana I had shipped to a private postal box, I collapse onto the pleather recliner and light up. Drawing it deep into my lungs, I let the pungent smoke settle over me as I slowly blow it out. When the relaxed buzz sneaks in on the edges, I fire up the laptop porn. I learned my lesson and this time I'm busting a nut before I hit the booze. And I want to find that man from the last video again.

Cueing up the video, I lounge naked with a joint in one hand and my dick in the other. The dark-haired man with the huge dick fucks *my* face and not some tiny blonde twink's. The twink is cute, but not my type. Letting my head fall back on the chair, I listen to the moans from the laptop speakers as I stroke myself. When I close my eyes, the dark and handsome man waits for me.

He's perfect.

Broad muscular shoulders, just the right amount of stubble, and mesmerizing blue eyes. It's his tongue on me, wicked and hot as he licks a path from my balls up to my cock. A groan leaves my lips, and I spread my legs wider. He buries his face there and I wish I had brought a toy out, because my imagination is on point tonight.

The joint tumbles from my fingers and I slide down farther, ignoring the squeak and pull of pleather on my ass as I shift. Coating my finger with spit, I tease myself before I give in and push inside. But it's not a finger inside my hole. It's the man with the dark hair filling me with his huge cock and it feels so fucking good. His satisfied smile peering down at me as he pumps draws a gasp from my lungs. It's so vivid I feel the drop of sweat from his brow hitting my chest. That's my tipping point and I shudder before coming on myself with a roar.

"Must be something in that weed. I swear I wasn't alone."

Still panting, I fumble around to find a discarded pair of underwear and mop up my mess.

I'm happy I skipped the gin tonight. Spent and noodle-like, I reach down and find the joint I dropped still smoking on the floor, and raise a shaky hand for a drag. I've never come that hard by myself before. And it was never so... real. I swear that guy was dicking me down in the flesh and not my imagination. Masturbation is fun and all, but I want to find men and lots of them.

How's that old saying go? Once you get a taste of the good stuff, you'll never want to use artificial again? Something like that, anyway.

My eyelids droop and I peel myself off the recliner to stagger into the bedroom. It's been a long day and I need to sleep.

After all, I get to do this again tomorrow.

"Yeah, like that. Swallow it all."

The suction is perfect. The heat is fucking amazing and the tongue on this man is out of this world. I'm going to come down his throat and not even warn him.

I grab a fistfull of his hair and shove him down farther on my hard cock and he doesn't even flinch. His blue eyes peer up at me, challenging me to go further and I do.

He just smiles around my dick and I don't know what he does, but whatever it is feels like my entire body just left earth and I'm soaring somewhere where the word bliss doesn't even begin to describe what I'm feeling.

"Holy shit. Holy shit."

If I wanted to warn him I was about to blow I couldn't have. It's the orgasm to trump all those before it and I lay there in a spent heap as he pops off my dick licking his lips.

"Good morning, Father."

My eyes fly open and I turn my head to the side quickly on the pillow to check out the other side of the bed.

It's empty.

With a shaking breath, I place my hand on my chest. That had to be the most vivid wet dream I've had since I was a kid. I could have sworn the same man from my masturbation session last night was here with me and swallowing my dick like he was a circus sword eater. The dried cum on my thigh is already pulling at my skin and I need to shower and move on with this day. No time for any debauchery just yet.

But I'm definitely cataloging that dream for later replays.

After I shower and dress, I pull out the bishop's letter and read the threats again. To remain silent as they fire me for crossing lines so many of us have before. A few even made bigger missteps than me and were just shipped away with a stern lecture about not letting it happen again. But you know what? Being a hypocrite is hard. I don't want to do it anymore.

I want to practice the most base of human behaviour and pursue happiness. Not some kind of notion of what happiness should be based on the pages of an ancient text that's open to misinterpretation. I want what makes me happy. Whatever brings a smile to my face and the whole body warmth of feeling truly content. I've lived in this moral castle for so long I almost forgot what it's like to do what I want simply because it brings me joy.

While what brings me most joy these days is porn, sex, and booze, I'm done feeling like a lesser human because of my tastes.

When the doorbell rings and Matthew lets himself in, calling out my name before I've even allowed him into my home, I'm beyond angry.

"Charles!" he barks, and I know he wants me to come running, but that's not happening.

Slowly, I exit the hallway, pulling a t-shirt on as he stands in the living room, jaw on the floor, surveying the mess I left behind last night.

Guess I should have made a better attempt to hide all that stuff. The lighter and marijuana still sit on the coffee table and the scent of it still hangs in the air. Matthew's face crumples like he swallowed sour milk, and it's funny for him to judge me like that.

"Do you always let yourself into houses that aren't yours?"

"It's church property, not yours, Charles."

"You know, I liked it better when you called me Charlie. Especially when you had your dick in my ass. You sounded all breathy and hot. It was nice."

His head snaps back as if I slapped him.

"What the hell is wrong with you?"

Flopping on the sofa, I noticed some dried jizz on the edge. Guess I really don't give a fuck anymore about this place.

"There's nothing wrong with me."

He should ask himself that question. He's the one who gives zero fucks about me after all we've done and said. Asshole.

"You're to be packed and out of this place today. That was the agreement."

"There was no agreement! You threw me under the bus to protect your own job! Your own.... you! That's not a fucking agreement!"

I want to stand right in his face and spray angry saliva on him. But I remain seated. I don't want to give him the pleasure of knowing I'm unraveling and he's the last thread to cut off and make it stop.

His cheeks turn red, and he at least has the decency to look embarrassed. He knows I'm right and this whole thing was never anything mutually agreed upon. A little voice inside still blames me, though. If I hadn't tried to be romantic and tell him how I felt, we wouldn't be here arguing.

"Charles. If you don't honour the letter, we're both going to look bad."

Ah, more confirmation it's only about him.

"So? Sounds like a you problem."

I chuckle as I pack up my laptop and make a show of stuffing the extra large bottle of lube inside.

"The only way you get the payout is to leave as agreed." He pulls an envelope from his pocket with a smug grin. "What's it gonna be?"

"Gee, Matt, let me think. I've got a few things to tie up and then I'm going to pack my shit and get out of here. Since I've discovered I really like gay sex and gin... oh, and that superb weed... I'm probably going to be unhinged for a while. I might have loose lips. I might not."

The blood drains from his face.

"And I have some savings so..."

"You promised." He seethes.

"Yeah, well, you promised you loved me and would never sell me out, so.... seems like a good trade."

He drops the envelope on the table and stomps to the door.

"If you're still here when I come by at 8PM tonight, that cheque will be canceled."

I give him the old middle finger salute.

"No problemo, Matt. You have a good day now."

The hollow silence now that I'm alone once again closes in. Sometimes it's too loud and I need to push the deafening quiet out of my head. Swallowing the lump in my throat, I wait for my breathing to return to normal.

There's still lots for me to accomplish before I leave here forever, and as much as I want to say I can't wait to get out of here, I'm... scared. This is like starting my life all over and while I'm elated to finally be myself, I'm going to be doing it alone. For the first time in thirty-five years.

My stomach growls and reminds me I still need to eat before getting the packing started. Time to raid the leftovers from that funeral and then get the fuck out of here.

DAVE

The door of my father's realm vanishes behind me and I'm left in a cramped closet in a church basement. Of course, I'm stuck in a *church* for the next seven days. I mean, what was I expecting? A week's stay at the Ritz-Carlton?

The closet is stuffy and small, with a box of older hymnal books shoved in the corner and a broken picture frame still with the painting of Jesus and his disciples in it. You just knew that would end badly when they needed a table for thirteen.

There's no noise outside the closet door and since it's early, and mid week, I'm likely here all alone. If anyone shows up, it would be a caretaker or maybe even the priest himself. If that happens, I'm sure I can handle either of them just fine.

Unfolding a chair I find wedged in the corner behind the broken painting, I gingerly sit and remove the demon handbook to review while I figure out my next steps. Flipping through the pages, I go back to basics and review the teachings I've known since I was a child.

Don't touch holy water.

Stay away from any kind of blessing.

Avoid Taco Bell.

You know, obvious stuff.

For several hours I browse the handbook and nothing jumps out as being completely out of the question for what I may or may not do. I can actually leave the church, so that's good to know. Again, there are rules to follow while in public, but I don't need to sit in the closet for a week. Which is indeed a good thing. I'm a big guy. Six foot five without the horns. Camped out in a closet for seven days would be, well, hell.

I'm about to skip to another section about the intricacies of human behaviour and how it relates to demons when the vision of a man pleasuring himself zings into my head. It's so crisp and clear I may as well be in the same room as him and watching a live show.

His green eyes bore into mine and he's breath-takingly handsome with curly blond hair framing his face in a golden halo. He's downright delicious in his sexual pose and this is one time I'm grateful to be tagged in someone's very vivid and sexual fantasies. Because he sees me too. He's so close I can taste the sweat on his brow as I lick my lips.

Is this the priest of this church? As I watch him chase his orgasm, I know when he senses me there as more than just his imagination, and that moment... well, it's... weird. In a good way, though, because he thought of me when he stuck his finger in his ass and came all over himself. I've never peeked in on someone like that before and stayed that long. It's always been brief flashes and then gone. But this was different.

I liked it.

I liked him.

He was definitely not someone to throw out of bed for eating crackers. Okay, not quite. I wouldn't be able to sleep in a bed full of crumbs, but I'd dustbuster around him and ask him to stay.

If he's the priest, he's probably the last person I should ask for help, but fuck, he's hot. The whole thing was hot. He was thinking of me. But I can't allow a pretty face to sidetrack me. I need to plan how to get through this week and return home. And I won't make part of the plan to include sex.

Nope.

Although, defiling a priest would probably be good, er, bad? Might earn me points with Dad. If I can work it in and not hurt the guy, I'll think about it.

With a sigh, I return to my manual and read the boring part I've always skipped. It's hard to understand human behaviour. There's so many complicated emotions. The longer I read, though, the more I think that maybe it's not so hard after all. It's actually relatable. This whole concept about me being too nice for a demon makes more sense now. There are a lot of pages about how humans try to bargain and appeal to your sense of empathy. Along with a note that it's easy for demons to ignore because we just don't have that capability.

But that's wrong.

The more I read about the various actions humans will do to spare their lives, the more I feel like I'm truly the horrible demon my father says I am. Because they all sound like me.

This will be harder than I thought. How can I be a proper demon when I relate to humans so much? I'm not perfect and neither are they. But I can understand the why of their actions. I just don't understand why I have to be the one so different.

Exhausted from all the information and the possibility I just wasn't born to be evil, I let my head rest against the wall and get some sleep before I start this week of what I'm sure will be a new kind of hell for me.

My eyes fly open, and I bolt upright on the flimsy folding chair with a gasp.

That man was in my dream. I *never* dream.

I've not even been here long enough to leave the damn church, and I'm already having weird things happen to me. This can't be a good sign for what's to come.

My stomach growls in the tiny closet, bringing me back to the present. I don't know if there's a huge time warp coming to earth or what, but it feels like I haven't eaten in a week. Food first and I'll consider what this dream might mean once my stomach is full. Hangry demons are not pleasant.

It's rare I'm drawn into someone's fantasy, but the few

times I have been, it's with mixed results. Again, I fail at the whole demon thing. I'm likely the only demon ever that has graciously talked someone out of sex and snuggled with them instead. Sometimes a hug is better, you know?

Although if this dude is as hot in person as he was in the dream, I might just take what he offers. And if he's the priest too, well, that's a hot fantasy for anyone, I think.

Hey, this is a good start to being bad, right? Taking advantage of a man of the cloth?

Gotta be.

My stomach growls again, and I unfold from the chair. Nudging open the little closet door, I listen for any noise of people and I straighten to my full height as I step out. My back cracks as I stretch myself out and I'm grateful I don't have to do that for a full week. It would wreck my back sleeping on that god awful chair for that long.

It's easy to find my way to the kitchen. My nose smells everything and I know the fridge has platters of cold cuts and all kinds of amazing, delicious things. Even in my world, we know food made by church ladies is possibly the best thing ever. My mouth waters just thinking about what kind of sandwich I can make and how many varieties of desserts I might find.

On my way to the kitchen, I poke my head into a few of the odd rooms and laugh at the children's area with its wildly inaccurate photos of my dad and his brothers. No wonder my dad hates churches so much. They can't even take the time to research and do a proper photo of Satan for pete's sake. His horns are way too small in this one. He'd be pissed with that painting and probably rip it right off the wall. We're very sensitive about our horn size.

Once I find the kitchen, I indeed discover all the cold cuts I thought I sniffed out and, with a happy hum, I lay all the goodies across the counter. This is going to be good. Oh! They have those tiny little pickles that are delish. I love those!

Swinging my hips to the tune in my head, I decide what to eat first. Since I'm an adult and can do what I want, I pop a few of those yummy dessert squares in my mouth. The lemon curd is so perfectly tart I'd like to think magic was involved.

After removing all the trays and searching around for the condiments, I do a little dance around the kitchen. Never underestimate the quality of church-made food. Maybe it's because it's made with love or maybe it's because it comes from some grandma's kitchen, but whatever makes it taste so good deserves a celebratory dance.

But before I make a sandwich, I need to find the restroom.

Even Demons have to take regular pee breaks

CHARLES

Just in case someone happens into the church, even though there's no mass or confessional scheduled, I put the damn collar and black shirt on before I hit the basement kitchen.

Some old habits die hard. It's not like the collar makes me a different person. It's just one more of those public image things the church loves. Heaven forbid Father Charles be seen in church looking like common folk.

Such a bunch of bullshit.

Before I head to the basement kitchen, I drag out the empty boxes I'd gathered last week to pack. Just like everything else, I had to keep that hidden, too. Nobody wanted questions about how come I was stockpiling boxes. Nobody wanted to tip off the parishioners I'd already given my last mass. I was to vanish without explanation, since that made it easier. Not for me, of course. But it sure did for everyone else.

I'm not exactly sure how I'm supposed to just vanish, but that's what I've been told to do. Since I'm hanging by a thread right now, I'll choose to follow along. Doesn't mean I'll not try to make it difficult for Matthew, though, if I can.

I was tempted to rub another one out this morning before getting to the packing I had to do. The image of the man from my dream last night just wasn't fading away. But of course, Matthew had to show up here and kill my erection with his holier than thou attitude that was quite repulsive. He's nothing but a hollow man with no care for the wellbeing of others. His complete lack of compassion for what happens to me took me by surprise and I almost wish I'd never met him.

How do I already despise the one I loved so fiercely? It's funny how sometimes we don't allow ourselves to see truths when they are plain as day. Love does that I've learned.

The door to the basement thunks closed behind me as I step out of the rectory and my bare feet slap on the tiled stairs. I chuckle to myself when I realize I took the time to wear my collar but not shoes. Leftovers from the funeral reception are calling my name and I'm taking advantage of the cooking skills of the ladies' auxiliary while I still can. The only thing better than church-lady-made food is a good joint and a better orgasm. I'll settle for one out of three for now. The other two I'll do my best to get to later.

When I enter the kitchen, its usual tidiness is nowhere to be seen. An odd combination of foods litter the counter. Platters of cookies, lunch meats and a mayonnaise bottle are spread out, like someone's midnight snack interrupted.

I don't have the patience to deal with this. I just wanted a small snack and maybe some of those Nanaimo bars I'd make a deal with the devil for. Placing the foil covers back over the food, muttering at the carelessness, I wonder how long it's been left out for and if the food's even still good to eat. Nothing will ruin my mood faster than being denied a sandwich on those homemade buns Mrs. Walker bakes.

The sound of a toilet flushing silences my inner musings and I'm frozen in place. Someone's still here. Footsteps travel across the empty gathering space, measured, purposeful and unhurried. I wait with hands on hips, annoyance ramping up, to see which of my parishioners, soon to be *former* parishioners that is, has been so rude to stay behind and eat food without asking.

The steps pause before entering the kitchen. A loud belch breaks the silence, and a man enters the doorway. Not just any man. A handsome man, with barely there scruff on his face and a perfectly tailored suit. A familiar man I saw last night when I dared to think I wasn't alone with my cock in my hand. My hand flutters to my collar with a gasp, and I make the sign of the cross. Another old habit I'll need to get rid of.

"Hey there, Father, sorry about the mess. I was going to clean up eventually." He moves towards the food as I back pedal, slamming my back into the oversized fridge.

"You're real," I whisper, mouth agape as I watch this apparition, the very one I imagined with his dick up my ass mere hours ago. And he's standing in front of me, popping coconut balls into his mouth like it's just another Saturday night at the movies.

He snorts. A thin puff of smoke rises from somewhere on

his body. "Of course I'm real. Why wouldn't I be real? You believe in some guy in the sky who can cure the sick—who never makes public appearances, I might add—but you don't believe in me?" He raises a pointed eyebrow in my direction before choosing a rice crispy square and leaning against the counter.

"That hurts. A little left of center." He rubs a spot over his heart. "I know what you were thinking about doing with me. I can't pretend that comment isn't hurtful."

He bites into the crispy treat with a low moan. "These women sure know how to bake, Padre. How are you not gaining weight with this here all the time?" He chews and swallows. "You look good, by the way. Better in person."

"How are you even here?" I still can't believe he's standing in the church kitchen. He's just a figment of my imagination, isn't he? A hot as hell porn star who happened to have a starring role in my wet dream this morning. Yet he's talking like he knows me. Has seen me before. Maybe that weed is better than I thought and I'm still imagining all of this.

He turns to rummage through the fridge and my gaze immediately falls to the amazing ass I thought was only a dream. But it seems pretty real right now. Even though I'm leaving the church, my ingrained beliefs roar to the surface.

He must be the work of the devil. Unless there is a god and he's sending me a parting gift of the most fuckable man I've ever laid eyes on.

I pinch my arm and yelp.

Yep, I'm awake and this is happening. Holy cheeseburgers.

He turns around with a plate of cold cuts. "Are you checking out my ass, Father?" He flashes a wicked grin before selecting several slices of meat, slapping them on the counter.

"I was looking for a tail, if you must know." Heat floods my cheeks and I tug at my collar. Not a good time to be suddenly shy. He's literally a man I want to bend me over the closest surface and bang me like a screen door in the wind. Not the sort of thing I should blurt out at first meeting, I don't think. Although, if he's real, and he was actually watching me when I fucked my hand, then he has to be...

"Ah yes, all demons should have tails. Common misconception, actually." He squirts a line of mayo on a slice of ham, covers it with a slice of roast turkey and takes a bite. "I don't have a tail, never have. You're welcome to take a closer look, Padre... I only bite if you want me to." He winks and keeps eating, devouring the sandwich like he's not been around food for years.

And, okay, my brain isn't computing, since I'm picturing him biting my ass, because he just said he's never had a tail, but I can check. Because he's a *demon*. And clearly this is something that shouldn't make me hard. Though the ache in my pants disagrees.

Holy Joseph and Mary. He *is* the work of the devil.

"How... how did you get here? I mean, you were someone I made up in my head. I'm having trouble understanding what's going on here."

Well, not totally made up. That guy in the orgy looked a lot like him. Power of suggestion and all that.

He finishes his disgusting tour of the cold cut platter and points a finger at me. "See, that's where things get a little dicey." He dusts off his hands and rummages for glasses in the cupboard while I let my mind go back to his look-alike in the video and lick my lips. "Funny story. See the coat closet down there?" He gestures to a door down the hallway off the kitchen. "That's not just a coat closet, it's the portal to my realm. My dad, who you might know, is one of Satan's underlings. And he thinks I haven't been doing a good job as a demon." He says that last part with finger quotes and uncorks a bottle of wine, pouring the rest into one glass with a frown.

He takes a sip from the glass covered in sunshine-yellow daisies and licks his lips. "Have you tried this wine? It's fan-freaking-tastic." He holds the glass out to me. "Go on, Father, just a sip."

"Call me Charles."

Why I'm telling a man who just told me he's a demon to call me by first name, I don't know. Maybe it's because I don't want to be called Father anymore. Maybe it's because I want him to moan my name later.

Probably a bit of both to be honest.

I take the glass and drink, never breaking eye contact and smile when I notice the way he shifts against the counter.

"So, why isn't your father happy with your demon ways?" I pass the wine glass back to him and our fingers brush. My dick jumps at the touch, reminding me I didn't take care of it earlier. He has nice hands too.

Draining the glass, he sets it on the counter and steps closer to me. "I'm here because my dad thinks I'm too nice. Whatever that fucking means. I mean, I'm not a monster, okay? It's not a bad thing to be a little friendly here and there."

His eyes glow a muted red as he speaks and a warmth radiates off his body. It's warm enough for the sweat to bead on my forehead just standing this close to him. And there's something else. Maybe it's a false feeling of intimacy since he was in my dream, or maybe it's because my dick is suddenly insatiable. Whatever it is, it's enough for me to want to be a total slut and beg him to fuck me in the church kitchen. Hell, maybe even eat some cookies afterwards. I still haven't got the Nanaimo bar I wanted yet.

"Did you find any more of that wine while you were in the fridge?"

He snorts. "You don't think I can make you more? That's not a trademarked party trick, you know." He smooths a palm across my cheek and his eyes soften along with his voice. "You're a good-looking guy. A man of honour in the church. Why are you thinking about fucking a stranger in the kitchen?"

"Is reading minds a power or something you have?"

He shrugs his shoulder. "Sometimes. I never really worked on the skill, but you're very... sensual. You're dialled into my channel, if you know what I mean."

I actually don't know what he means because real life demons who walk on two legs in fitted suits and, dear god, have *horns* sprouting from their head are not supposed to be real.

But when life presents opportunities, take them. Maybe even grab them by the horns, if appropriate.

"So... if I wanted you to fuck my face right here, would you do it?"

Dave

Charles's words don't shock me. After what I saw last night, his boldness is not unexpected. However, my reaction isn't one he will like.

Should I take advantage and use this man who is supposed to be of higher moral values than me in the kitchen of the church basement while a portrait of Jesus watches?

I should.

It would be very demon-like if I did.

I mean, I want to, but... I need to slow his roll.

But maybe only a little.

"So, this is one of those awkward moments where I say yes, but tack on too many conditions for the sake of propriety."

His brow furrows as he pins me with those gorgeous green eyes. The annoyed flush to his cheeks is quite appealing. It really draws attention to his pretty eyes.

"You're gonna have to explain because I don't know if you picked up on my channel," he uses finger quotes like I did and it's super cute, "but I'm about to be an *ex*-priest and I have roughly twelve hours to pack my shit and get out of here thanks to my asshole ex, and you're the guy I fantasized about last night and this morning. I'm literally hard just standing in the room with you. It would be nice to deal with it and forget my issues for a short time."

I flick my eyes to the tent in his pants. Huh, he's not lying, and that's a decent package he's hiding. For a human, anyway. Talk about flattering.

"Do we need to negotiate?"

"Negotiate? It's not a hostage situation. I'm literally asking you to use me so I can get off. What do you want to negotiate?"

"Remember the bit about me being a demon and not that good at it?" He motions for me to continue. "Well, this is one of those times."

"So, you don't want to put your dick in my mouth because what? Because you have issues with casual sex?"

I take another coconut ball and chew to buy some time to reply. It's not just that, but I've had no one question me like this before. I've never had to explain it out loud.

"I can't just have my way with you."

"Why not!?"

He stomps his foot like an angry toddler, and it's adorable.

"Because I have to like, know something about you first. Safe sex talk, define the relationship, you know... that stuff."

He mutters under his breath.

"This is why people choose dildos. No negotiating and defining. Down for a fuck whenever you need. Zero drama."

He's not wrong. I've been there too. But I can't just

randomly tell this person I'm a cuddleslut, and fuck and run isn't my style. Even though he's as tempting as this tray of baked goods. I'd love to devour him like all these treats I can't seem to get enough of.

Turning to the counter, I lift a chocolate chip cookie off a tray. "If you don't want to at least talk some first, and need to come so badly, why don't you do it yourself? Just like you did last night."

His eyes darken. "Are you into voyeurism or is this just you being nice?"

I tilt my hand back and forth. "Both?"

With a smug grin, he unzips and lets his pants fall to the floor and my sensitive nose picks up the scent of his pre-cum. I pretend not to care and munch on my cookie. He steps out of his underwear, then his shirt and collar, and stands there butt fucking naked with his cock jutting out, proud as can be. He's stunning. And I want to backtrack on my earlier words and bend him over the table. However, I want to know what he's going to do next even more.

His gaze darts to my head, and I know he's noticed my horns popping out. They aren't enormous, but when I'm turned on or angry, I sometimes can't keep them locked down. For any normal human, it's scary, but the heat in Charles's eyes makes me think he likes it.

Propping a foot on the chair next to him, his defiant gaze never leaves my face as he strokes himself for me. I want to do the same, but I'm enjoying this too much, so I settle for rearranging myself instead. He pops an eyebrow, clearly noticing I'm enjoying the show. When he sucks his finger into his mouth, making it all spit slick, I know what he intends. His fantasy from last night where he wished that finger was my dick. My breath hitches as he shows himself no mercy. Plunging his digit in so fast it has to be painful. I can't bear to watch him continue.

"Stop."

My voice booms in the small area, and he waits for my instruction. He won't enjoy it like that and he shouldn't be so rough with his body. My gaze lands on the little pats of margarine they put on the buffet tables and that will do better than nothing. He remains in place, chest heaving as I first smear the margarine on my fingers and then onto his raw hole.

His body jolts when my fingers skim across the sensitized flesh.

"Go ahead, Charles. Finish yourself. You should enjoy it more like this."

Good lord, he just goes for it and jacks himself off with his buttered up fingers buried in his ass. I couldn't look away if I wanted to, but the intensity in his eyes pins me in place and does more than just grow my erection.

This is a performance for me. And I'm torn between watching and taking part.

"You're a dirty little thing aren't you? Come for me, gorgeous. I want to see you come undone."

His orgasm hits hard and fast. With a moan, he spills into

his fist and I can't tear my eyes away from the mess of cum on his dick and hand. His chest heaves with short, ragged gasps. Those pretty lips part with every pant and he continues to keep his beautiful green eyes locked on me.

I reach for another cookie to settle my racing heart and give me something to do with my hands that doesn't involve touching my very hard cock. Or grabbing his head and kissing him until he tells me to stop.

"Charles! Are you down there?"

His eyes widen as he looks to the doorway. I know it shouldn't matter who it is, because at no point would it ever be good to be caught in the church kitchen naked with cum all over yourself. In no story will that ever end well. But the other man's voice sets me on edge and I know it means terrible things for Charles if I don't help.

"Grab your clothes and hide in that pantry. I'll tell you when to come out." I whisper as I shove his clothes into his hands.

Thankfully, he does as he's asked and I watch his ass jiggle as he does this little waddle type walk with his clothes in one hand and cum-filled hand in the other.

Conjuring a quick boner killing scene to tame my erection, and also to help withdraw my horns, I step out of the kitchen and right smack into some pompous-looking clown.

"I'm so sorry. Are you okay?" I ask.

He's not thrilled, that's for sure. And he's a small dude. Of course, everyone seems small to me, but he's tilted his head back to make eye contact. He's shifty. I immediately don't like him.

"I'm looking for Charles. Who are you?"

"Oh, I'm a friend of his from long ago. He just stepped out. Something about needing more boxes to pack with. I didn't know he was leaving the church. How terrible."

I've gently steered him to face back where he came and lead him farther from the kitchen. With a look over my shoulder, I watch Charles make a scamper to the door leading back upstairs, and I cough to cover the sound of the door closing behind him.

"Uh yes, it's terrible. He'll leave a giant hole in the parish. What did you say your name was?"

"Ah, yes. Holes are hard to climb out of. Especially when you dig it yourself. Am I right?"

We've arrived back at the stairs leading him up to the church and I block the doorway so he can't look behind me. "You have a great day, Matthew. I'll tell him you dropped by."

His eyes narrow as he studies me closer.

"I didn't tell you my name."

"You didn't have to."

Again, he inspects me closer. I'm a nice guy. Too nice. It's why I'm in this mess, but this man is close to meeting a real demon. The scary kind. I know what he's thinking and Charles doesn't need this asshole in his life.

"But I —"

"Toodle loo."

I push him through the doorway and pull the door closed,

fake smiling real big and watching to make sure he heads up the stairs. He does, but not until he takes out his cell phone and places a call.

I wonder if this is one of those times I should have just done the whole blazing eyes routine and fucked with him a bit?

Probably.

But it's taken care of, and now I need to find that freaky little priest and make sure he's okay.

Because like it or not, I can't help myself.

I kind of care what happens to him.

And doesn't that just fuck up the whole reason for me being here?

CHARLES

As soon as Matthew was far enough away and occupied by... shit, I don't even know the tall drink of water's name.

A damn demon.

Doesn't matter. He provided the diversion so I could get back up to the rectory. What the hell did Matthew even bother coming back here for, anyway? Did he just want to make it even more crystal clear I have no home or job past 8 PM tonight?

My ass cheeks are still slippery with margarine and the cum drying on my pubic hairs has moved past the mild irritation phase and into the 'please shower now' phase. I should want to scrub the surface layer of my skin off because of the shame of what I just did.

I asked a complete stranger to fuck my face in the church kitchen. And when he declined, I masturbated in front of him. It was a thrill. I won't lie about how much I loved it. Showing off for a sexy man who was clearly interested, even though he chose to eat cookies over me.

Mark that down as yet another thing I never thought I'd do. Seems like I'm one of those *give them an inch and they take a mile* type of people. And I need to kick the feelings of shame to the curb. Discovering your sexual preferences and appetite later in life is never a bad thing. Even if it is in church.

Will he know I'm up here and let himself in? Will he want me to relieve him now? My spent cock twitches with the thought and I pause once outside the door to the rectory.

Oh fuck, I hope so. Those horns on his head grew along with the cock in his pants the longer he watched me.

But he also said some things that make zero sense to me. He's the poster child of all things immoral. Yet he doesn't want casual sex. And something about not being a good demon. None of this makes any sense and I'll need chemical assistance to get through the rest of this day. It's not even noon and I already want to smoke up.

The door closes behind me and I pause at the half-full (hurrah for optimism!) bottle of gin on the counter. Shaking my head at the early hour, I head to the shower and bypass the booze for now. The demon will know where to find me. Apparently, I'm on his channel and I think that might work in my favour. I won't address the fact he's not human for now. That little morsel can be conveniently ignored for as long as I need.

But that was a close call, with Matthew showing up. I'm not even sure why he did. He dropped off everything earlier. I know when I need to leave and I know what I will or won't do about it as well. Although, it would have been nice to see Matthew's face walking in on me while blowing some rando in the kitchen.

Dammit, I didn't even get the snack I wanted when I went down there. Ah well, not the first time I chose sex over food, and probably won't be the last. Funny how your priorities can change when the proper options present themselves and you finally know what you've been missing your whole life.

Ditching my dirty clothes in the bedroom first, I turn on the shower and pull my thoughts back to thinking about what I need to pack, so I get out of here in the few short hours I have left.

A pang of disappointment settles when I remember the Cook family are scheduled to baptize their little boy tonight. As much as I hated forcing myself to do most parts of this job I didn't agree with, the Cooks are a nice family. Daniel even has a gay brother he chose as the child's godfather and I genuinely liked the meetings with all of them. I'm letting them down by walking away.

Scrubbing my hair harder than necessary, I realize that's all my life is. One big let down for other people.

Hey, Charles, did you get the scholarship? No, my GPA was too low.

Hey, Charles, did Susan say yes to a date? No, she said I'm not her type.

Oh, Charles, did you water the plants while we were gone? No, I'm sorry, I was busy and forgot.

Oh, Charles, did you talk the rich parishioner into writing a cheque to fix the church roof? Yes! Because he asked if I could blow him for that much money and, of course, I said I'd do it in the Lord's name.

I still got shit on when I delivered the cheque because it wasn't as much as they wanted. So I'm always full of disappointment. And something inside me hurts when I think about it.

Turning off the shower, I reach for my towel and screech when someone standing there hands it to me.

"I nearly had a heart attack! Next time, announce you're in the room."

"Like with trumpets or something?"

"Just... don't sneak up on me next time."

"Oh, so there's a *next time* I get to walk into the bathroom and hand you a towel while you're dripping wet naked?"

I scrub the towel over my skin as he stands there, assessing me with his dancing blue eyes. I'm not sure if he's joking, to be honest, so I choose to ignore the question. If he hasn't figured out that he can have me naked, wet or dry, anytime or place, he might be too dense for me to deal with.

"Matthew was looking for you."

"Mmm, I heard. Thanks for getting rid of him for me."

"You're welcome. Now, what's this about needing to pack and leave?"

Tossing the towel on the counter, I squeeze past him back to my room, and he trails behind me like a puppy.

"Well, Matthew, is the guy making me leave. You see, we were involved, and it was getting a little dicey for him to be found out. He wants to keep his reputation immaculate, right? So he's kicking me out and bribing me before I have time to tell my story."

He opens his mouth to speak, but I hold up a hand. "Listen, he's an asshole. I know that, but like, I'm getting out of here. I should have done it years ago."

Rummaging through my dresser, I pull out a pair of clean underwear before emptying the rest of the drawer into the suitcase on my bed.

"And I won't let him force me to do anything else to make him look good. I'm a little tired of it, you know?"

Hopping on one foot while I tug the underwear on, I notice his eyes trained on me and oof... it's not fucking possible for me to be horny again so soon. Like biologically, I mean. But...

"You never told me your name," I say, instead of thinking of him purring *my* name across his lips as he comes.

He hands me a t-shirt from the pile on the bed and looks away. Is he... nah, he can't be embarrassed. Is he?

"Uh, it's Dave."

"Dave. Not Satan or Lucifer or something more sinister?"

"Well, those are already taken, so I'm just Dave."

"Excuse me, *just Dave*, you're not just anything. What's your dad's name?"

"Does it matter?"

"No. I'm just curious."

He clears his throat, shifting as he stuffs his hands in his pockets.

"Listen, Charles, I, ah, sort of need your help."

Pausing at the closet, I turn my head his way.

"I'm listening, Dave."

Ugh, my voice still takes that pious tone I used for confessional and I hate it. But Dave's shoulders relax and even though I'm in a hurry to get out of here, I can't ignore how he seems to need someone to listen to him.

Sitting on the bed, I tap it gently in invitation, and he takes it. Reaching into his suit coat, he pulls out a small, very worn book with a sigh.

"Promise you won't laugh."

"You just watched me jerk off and smeared margarine on my ass to do it. I think we're way beyond the embarrassment factor here."

He shifts his gaze my way, and the temperature rises in the room. His nostrils flare and little pointy nubs show themselves on this head. It's cute. Reminds me of the catfish I used to catch as a kid.

"Right, and we're going to come back to that, but first I need your help." He flips open the tiny book and stops at a dog-eared page. If that's not a literary crime, I don't know what is. "I was trying to figure out what I can do when I leave the church. I'm supposed to avoid anything holy, so I should probably get out of here. But, um, I mentioned I'm not a good demon. Like I'm so good it's bad." He sighs and it sort of

breaks my heart. "My father sent me here to learn to be more…
like you, I guess? As a demon, I'm pretty sucky."

Gently, I take the tiny book from his mammoth hand and
flip through the pages.

"I'm sorry, but is this a handbook on how to be a demon?
You have an etiquette to follow on how to be evil?"

"Sort of? I mean there are rules, right? But they're more like,
*don't do this unless you want to never return to the underworld
because you're dumb*, rules."

"So, what do you need my help with, Dave?"

"Uh, well, you're kind of not that holy anymore, right? I
don't know much about you yet, but you're a priest who broke
his vows. And it seems like you've done a lot more stuff that
isn't very priest-like. So… maybe you could teach me how to
be like that?"

I don't know what hurts me more. The fact a demon just
asked me to teach him how to be bad or the fact I want to.
Or something entirely different that I don't want to give any
headspace to because I know it won't be pretty when I do.

"So, is there stuff you can't do? Ultimate rule you can't break
or anything I should know?"

"Mostly church stuff. Like don't get blessed or touch the
holy water. Just the usual stuff they tell you in movies." He
smiles at me and it's charming. Beautiful even. I bet his smile
helps to get whatever he wants.

"Okay, well, does me saying *oh god* when we have sex count
as a blessing or is that okay?"

His eyebrows shoot up as I chuckle to myself. That one was too easy.

"Right. I don't think so, no. Unless you plan to make the sign of the cross while you do it, I think I'm okay."

He paces across the small room and picks up a teddy bear from the top of my dresser. It was a gift from a little girl on the anniversary of my first year in the parish. She told me I should keep it for company and I did. Now Dave strokes it with a tiny smile on his face. It's a shame I have to give him some bad news when he seems so at ease.

"Um, so, I don't know how to say this, but it's customary to bless the meals at church. That includes the luncheon food for the funeral service. So while not technically communion, it was blessed."

I wince when he gasps and sits back down next to me.

"So I already fucked up one of the biggest rules they have? What if I can't go home now?"

"Maybe there's a loophole?" I offer, but I'm not totally convinced.

Picking up the book I had placed on the bed, I flick through the pages of his demon handbook and wonder where my life took such a dramatic turn.

"Oh! Look at this!" Pointing to the passage in the back under exceptions, I run my finger across the words of importance as I read aloud. "Should any demon find themselves in violation of any code, they have one chance with a meeting to clear their name. The representatives of the Circle of Satan, as per their availability, will decide the outcome."

Dave purses his lips in thought.

"So if I break rules, I can appeal with their discretion?"

"That's what it seems like, yes. But didn't you say your father sent you here to be more... bad? How is following rules a good thing for you? Doesn't it seem counterproductive?"

His full lips dip into a frown, and not for the first time since he showed up, I wish I knew how his lips felt stretched over my cock.

"You think if I break the code rules, that's more bad than following them?"

"Well, look at me. I'm supposed to be celibate and we both know that's not the case. I'm also supposed to avoid a bunch of other things that turned out to be fantastic. But I'm not doing that either. I've broken at least four of the really important rules. That put me out of a job and I'm... disgraced."

I say the last bit with finger quotes and wiggle my eyebrows. I'm hoping to make him laugh, but he's clearly still distressed about not being good at what he does and letting down his father.

"Listen, you seem to have this whole bad thing covered way better than I do. Teach me to do that. I want to break the rules. Or follow the rules. I'm getting confused." He runs a hand through his jet black hair. "I was never good at tests."

Snapping the handbook closed, I toss it on the floor and rake my eyes over him.

"How bad do you want to be?"

Boldy, I place his hand on my crotch and thrill at the sudden wave of heat in the small bedroom. If he sends off waves of heat whenever he's aroused, heating bills will go way down. That's another perk to keeping him around. Real money saver during Canadian winters.

His lips tilt in a salacious grin. *Finally*, he's onboard with the debauchery and my entire body shivers despite the heat wave.

"As bad as banging a priest in nothing but his collar." His fingers give a small squeeze and I whimper. "Will you do that, Charles?"

"I'll do whatever you ask me to."

He snaps the waistband of my briefs. "Take this off, get your collar, and get on your knees."

Fucking yes. Yes, please, because I may be dirty, but I'm always polite.

I can't move fast enough. Running back out to the living room, I find my collar on the floor where I tossed it and slip it on while attempting to remove my boxers in a full on run. Stumbling into my bedroom, I pull up at the doorway with a gasp.

"Holy shit. Maybe there is a god."

Dave, the demon from Heaven because there's no way he's from Hell, stands before me naked with a cock so big I'm not sure it will even fit in my mouth, let alone any other orifice. And yet I'm aching for it.

Dropping to my knees just like he asked, I tilt my head back and open my mouth in invitation.

"Wait. Stand up."

He reaches for me, eyebrows knitted together. His sizzling hand grips my elbow, pulling me up closer.

"I know you're freaky, and we already did the kitchen jerk thing. That was hot, by the way. But... I can't just shove my dick in your mouth."

"I literally want you to, Dave. Just do it. Be bad."

Blue balls will kill me with all his indecision.

His eyes search mine and the internal war plays across his face. He wants to do this and I don't know how else to convince him it's okay.

Slowly, I kneel before him again and open my mouth in invitation.

"I want you to, Dave. You have my permission. I'm begging you. Use me like I'm dying for you to."

With a guttural moan, he slides the tip of his giant dick across my lips.

Firm hands on the side of my face hold me in place, and his thumb brushes gently over my cheek.

"Tap my leg if I'm too rough," he murmurs and his tender gaze for me makes me slam my eyes closed.

I nod yes and lean closer, stretching my lips over his hot, hard cock. I'm still new at this whole giving a blow job thing, but Dave makes me feel like I'm a damn professional cocksucker with the sounds he's making.

"Fuuuck... Charles..."

Dave uses me like I asked. Finally. As his mammoth cock hits the back of my throat, gagging me, he tries to pull away, but I press farther, determined to overcome the natural response of my body. His grip on my head softens and I advance, taking the control from him and swallowing his length until I can't breathe.

The filthy sounds Dave keeps making fulfills my filthiest dreams. To hear him so unraveled because of me is the ultimate trip. And a complete turn on.

I swallow more and I can't breathe.

With my nose firmly buried in his patch of curly pubic hair and his hot thick cock wedged in my throat, black dots dance at the edge of my vision and I'm oddly at peace with the feeling of impending unconsciousness. My own balls grow tight listening to Dave's moans and I don't know how much longer I can hold out.

But he answers the question for me when he pulls my mouth off his cock with a shout and shoots his hot load all over my face. Gulping in a much needed breath to my burning lungs, I lick my lips. Not sure what I was expecting, but his cum tastes like honey.

"Oh, I'm so sorry. I should have warned you. Are you okay?"

With my eyes screwed shut, his fingers carefully wipe away the mess so I can open them.

"Don't apologize. I wanted it."

My voice is scratchy and thick, sore from having my throat battered.

His eyes drop to my groin and that deviant smile, the one

he could use to charm the pants off a... well, a priest, returns. "Seems you liked it."

The puddle of jizz cooling around my balls confirms this.

"I did." I stretch open my jaw and massage along my muscles. "You're pretty big, though."

I want to stand and clean up for the second time in as many hours, but he drops to his knees in front of me.

"I hurt you. You should have said something."

Expertly, his warm fingertips massage my jaw and again, his concern makes my chest tight. I push him away and stand quickly.

"You're supposed to be learning to be more demon-like. Take from me. Like it. Don't worry about how I feel."

Even I don't like how it sounds coming out of my mouth, but it's what he needs. He doesn't need to be gentle and doe-eyed.

I remove the collar from my neck, covered in demon cum, and toss it at him.

"Congratulations. You've cum on the cloth of the Lord. That outta win you points with Dad."

Spinning on my heel, I head to the shower before I allow myself to dwell on the fact he may actually care about how I feel.

Dave

"So what exactly is your plan?"

Charles has been wandering his place half naked and throwing things in boxes all mish mash since the epic blow job he gave me earlier. I've been with a lot of men and women and no one has ever swallowed me like Charles did.

Does a mind-altering orgasm change your perspective on life?

Yes. Yes, it does.

But so does a priest who is obviously spiralling out of control with this life. Being more demon like and less sensitive is no longer top of my agenda. Well, it sort of is. But I want to know what happened to Charles for him to be like this. He's more troubled than me. Which I know because, like the visions that have flashed in my brain like camera flashes, there's also been bursts of emotions. Feelings that don't seem to match with the person in front of me.

Somewhere along the way, I stopped listening to all the bad stuff that found its way into my brain and I only focused on the good things. Rather than turn people's fears into reality, I bucked the expected and put their fears to rest. It's likely the reason I'm in the mess I am now and facing being expelled from the underworld. It's not just my last bargain for daily bunny photos.

Charles needs someone. He's still confident on the outside and extremely, ah, sexual, but he's lost. I can't just let him go adrift like this and fall apart when I might be just what he needs to find himself again.

"I don't have a solid plan. The bishop said I had to leave by tonight, so I'm taking what I think I need and getting the fuck out of here."

He holds up an apron with *Kiss the Cook* on it.

"Do you wear an apron when you cook?"

"Uh, no. Do you?"

He tosses the apron aside with a shrug. "Not really. I wore it once to see if it would work. You know, kiss the cook?" He pulls more kitchen towels from a drawer and throws a few into the box. "It worked the first time."

His eyes blink faster and he turns away, staring into a kitchen cupboard with various cups and glasses.

"Charles?"

He shakes his head in response to my question and wordlessly brushes by me. The door to the bathroom closes, a loud snick in the already too quiet apartment.

This demon shit is hard. I'm not like my brothers.

I should drink his alcohol, eat his food, fuck him until he begs me to stop and leave without saying goodbye. It's all right here in front of me on a fucking silver platter.

But I can't.

With a sigh, I take a seat on the couch and spot the half-smoked joint on the table nearby. Charles is travelling down a self destructive road if the empty liquor bottles in the closet are any sign. Thank god he doesn't have a pet. I'd never make it back home if he had some adorable dog wagging around.

But the lack of an animal wouldn't matter, anyway. I'm compelled to be with Charles in a weird way that I don't even understand. I only want to comfort him from the troubles he's clearly having issues coping with. Maybe even protect from more if I can.

My phone vibrates in my pocket and when I read the name of the caller, a cold sweat covers my brow.

"Hey, Dad. What's up?"

I cringe at my choice of words. Already off to a bad start.

"What's up? You ask me what's up when I've sent my youngest son to earth for the biggest trial of his life?"

"Sorry, Dad."

The sigh of a thousand regrets crosses the phone.

"Son. This is the only call I'm giving you. Ask anything. There's no help after this."

"I thought even you had to always be cruel. Why help me?"

"You're still my son. But this is the only chance you have for another six days. Is there anything you need to know?"

My eyes flick to the bathroom door that's still closed and if

Dad is serious, now's my chance to ask.

"What if I already broke a rule?"

"Dave, seriously?"

Pacing to the kitchen, I pluck the *Kiss the Cook* apron off the chair where Charles tossed it. He's totally kissable.

"Well Dad, you sent me to a church, and I was hungry and it sort of just happened."

"What happened exactly?"

"I ate blessed food and had sex with a priest."

The silence drags on so long I almost think he's hung up on me until he speaks again.

"You realize you've been there a full twenty-four hours, right?"

"Yeah, but I was hungry, and he's really cute. You should see how pretty his eyes are. They're kind of greenish? And he's blonde with these adorable curls. And that thing I can do where I see what they're thinking happened! So, I, ah... we had a drink and stuff."

"Listen, Dave. I don't think me checking in or prolonging this conversation is going to change anything. But I'm texting you the contact number of a guy I made a deal with once. If you need anything while you're there, call him."

"Okay. So, about the rule thing. Do I get to appeal or whatever the book says?"

Another long pause.

"Call me when your days are up. Goodbye, Dave."

The line goes silent in my hand and a moment later, a text

comes through from my dad with the number for someone named Mike. I save it to my contacts and wonder when I should call him. If Dad's tone was anything to go by, my chance of returning home is slim. And I only just got here.

The bathroom door is still closed, and a weird ache fills my chest. Why do I care so much if he's okay? This is worse than the guy with the pet rabbit.

Decision made, I rap my knuckles on the door.

"Charles? Are you okay?"

The door knob turns and when the door opens, the ache I was ignoring returns.

Red-rimmed eyes peek up from under his blonde curls.

"What's wrong? Can I help?"

I reach for him wanting to brush a stray tear from his cheek, but I let my hand drop. I pop the top button on my shirt instead so it's not so tight.

"I'm fine. Just needed a minute." He looks at his wrist where he'd normally have a watch. "I need to finish packing and get out of here. If you want to come with me..."

He leaves the words hanging, allowing me time to insert an answer.

"Yes. I do."

With a firm nod, he walks past me again.

"Then let's get shit done and leave this fucking place behind."

Charles packed little that wasn't personal property. Which was good because he had a lot of stuff. After we shoved it all in his very swanky Escalade, I got a lecture on how it wasn't his choice for a vehicle. Apparently it was a very generous gift from the diocese for his tireless efforts to build the faith.

He used air quotes and a snarky tone. I'm sure there's more to it than that, but it's what we have to drive.

Charles pulls his very nice Cadillac to a stop in front of the sleaziest motel I've ever seen. The light is out above the entrance and there's a crack in the glass by the door. The parking lot appears to be around the side of the building and there's one small yellow safety lamp glowing. The building next door has boards over the windows and doors as well.

I come from the suburbs of Hell, and this place gives me the creeps.

"You want to stay here tonight? You sure?"

I'm even worried about my safety. Broken street lights and shadows move in the depths. With a car like this, it's likely to be stripped the moment we go inside. Possibly sooner.

"I don't want to spend all my money right away and I don't know where else to go."

"Charles, the Walmart parking lot is better than this."

Movement from the corner of my eye sends the hairs on my neck up.

"Do as I say. Turn the key and get us out of here before you no longer have a vehicle."

When the car roars back to life, the headlights flood what I expected. Looters, likely gang members, were waiting to pounce and the glint of metal from the closest one sends my pulse into overdrive. Charles won't be safe here.

Charles squeaks but mercifully has the sense to gun the SUV and peel out of the parking lot before we become a crime statistic. He drives until we're back onto the main streets and no longer in the city's underbelly. While that motel was a place I would belong to as a demon, now that I've broken rules, I'm not sure if that's still the case. But one thing for sure is it's no place for Charles.

Finally, he pulls into a Walmart parking lot and rests his head on the headrest.

"I chose that place because a parishioner told me it was owned by their family. It was a safe place, I thought. They're good people."

"You sure about that? Even I didn't feel safe there."

"I'm not sure of anything anymore." He rubs the bridge of his nose. "Seems like nobody is who they say they are."

"I know a guy... well, my dad sent me the name of someone I could ask for help. I'll call him."

"Do you trust your dad? What if this guy is just a setup for you to fail?"

While the thought has already crossed my mind, I don't believe my dad would do that. If he truly wanted me to suffer, he would have already done it. In his own way, he's being kind to his son while keeping his bad ass image alive. I respect that and see my dad in a new light now.

Besides, can I fail any worse than I am now? I already care about what happens to Charles. That's the single worst thing to happen to a guy like me. And by guy, I mean demon. We don't care about anyone other than ourselves and a few demons in our family. This whole thing isn't right.

"I trust him. I'm going to call."

On the second ring, Mike picks up.

"Hello?"

"Hi, Mike? My name is Dave, and my dad gave me your number. He said I should call you if I ever need anything."

"And who's your dad, Dave?"

"Uh, Faustus."

"Ah, well, I'm at your service. What do you need?"

"A safe place to stay. And I have a friend."

I dart a glance at Charles. His eyes are closed, but I know he's listening. He's a friend, though. I mean, what else can he be?

"Is the friend a priest named Charles by chance?"

"Uh, yes."

"I'm going to text you an address. Drive there and park at the carport on the side. Wait until you hear from me before going in."

He ends the call and a moment later, my phone buzzes with an address. Charles turns to me.

"So? What's the new plan since I completely failed at mine."

"I have an address and he's meeting us there. I'm assuming it's safe, and he already knew I was with you."

He turns the key, and I enter the address into his GPS.

"It says it's a forty-five minute drive. Would you mind stopping for food somewhere first?"

"Yeah, I could eat. Do you care where?"

"What's your favourite?"

When Charles smiles, he's truly a beautiful man. It transforms his serious face into one that's boyish and full of easy going charm.

"There's this place called The Burger Barn. They have the best burgers ever. I haven't been for ages. Do you like fries? I'll share one with you."

"That sounds perfect. I love fries!" I really do. I'm likely far too excited for us to enjoy a dinner together. We have to eat after all. But I can't stop the next question before it rolls off my tongue. "Is it considered a date if we share food?"

His smile drops and I wish I hadn't said it.

"I'd rather not label it anything. We're just... it's just eating burgers. Nothing more than that. Just because you've already seen me naked covered in cum doesn't mean dates have to happen. Let's just... be casual."

I let his words steep in my brain. His fingers flex and unflex on the steering wheel, and I'm smart enough to notice this isn't about me and my choice of words. I shouldn't even care.

Yet my fingers itch to turn his face to me and tell him he's mine. Call it fate or karma or whatever else. We're likely stuck together for eternity. Or however long he lives, at least. Charles holds the key for me to find myself. It stings for him to push me away so fast.

Yeah, I watched him jerk himself and yes; I had my cock in his throat already. But maybe I'm a backward old-fashioned idiot. I just want to date the guy and get to know him better.

"Yeah, sure. Casual burgers. I'm fine with that."

I'm not really fine, but I'll make it work.

He nods, and the silence hangs in the SUV. It's suffocating and I can't stay quiet.

"You don't cover your fries in ketchup, do you?"

"What? Eww. No. Vinegar and salt. Sometimes gravy."

"Gross. At the same time? Don't they get soggy?"

"No, not at the same time. But yes, they can get soggy. I like them that way."

"I prefer a crispy fry."

He raises an eyebrow, and his lips tilt up again. Just a bit. But I'll take it.

"We'll split the fries before any condiments get added. How's that?"

"Sounds like a compromise. I'll take it."

He finds a parking spot at the Burger Barn and as we walk to the door together; I beat him to it and hold it open for him.

He might not want to call it a date, but I'm going to treat it like one.

Charles

"**G**reat choice, Charles. That was an amazing dinner."

The Burger Barn was always my go to when I wanted to eat my feelings. I've come here many times over the last few months. While I don't regret my decision to break free and live my life, the guilt is still there. All the people I've let down. Again.

And now I have this six foot five, blue eyed adonis along for the ride. Not sure how that happened, but it's unsettling. After Matthew smashed my heart and hope of a normal life to smithereens, I wanted nothing more to do with relationships. Not that this is a relationship, but I guess we can say we're friends, at least.

I just want to fuck anything that offers and drown myself in gin. Smoke some of that amazing weed I bought and just do whatever the hell I want. Preferably as often as possible. But Dave is... nice.

"Yeah, best burger for whatever ails you."

"What is it that ails you, Charles?"

Dave's smooth voice settles over me like a fuzzy blanket.

Those blue eyes aren't cold either. They're soft and warm like he cares. They make my heart pound faster.

"That's a loaded question."

"I've got time to listen."

His lips tilt, crooked and cute, and I realize he's mimicking how I listened to him earlier. I suppose it's only fair to share a little more since he did.

"I don't know what to do now. From the seminary to the church, I've followed structure and rules. Someone was always telling me what to do or say." I tidy the sugar packets in the dish, making all the writing face the same way. "When I was ordained, it was the same thing. Lots of rules and stuff. Never a moment to really do what I wanted. I had vacation days, but it seemed the diocese was always short somewhere and they shuffled me all over to cover."

My throat clicks as I reach for my glass of water. Now that I've started talking, it's like I can't seem to stop.

"I've never had time for me to just be Charles, the guy who likes to lie in bed and read late. Or the guy who likes to linger over his pancakes and coffee. I always miss Sunday football and I..."

I let my voice trail off because the last time I spoke about this, Matthew made me feel so small, so ridiculous, for even putting a voice to it.

"You what? You can tell me."

My voice is a whisper. "I want to be loved. In the open. With a real partner, not this I'm married to the church crap. I want someone to be proud of me as Charles, not Father Charles. Just me." I tear my gaze from the sugar packets and meet his again. "I just want to be a gay man and not be judged for it."

Dave stares back at me, and my chest rises with short puffs. Matthew didn't get it. He was perfectly fine living two lives. It didn't bother him to do it. He didn't have the same needs I did. There was no conflict for him because he felt work came first. Even when work was the one who made you stay quiet about who you really were.

"I certainly don't judge you for any of that. Doesn't everyone just want to be themselves without judgment? Without fear of what their families think when you might be a little different."

He reaches across and squeezes my hand. "Us outcasts need to stick together."

The server stops at our table and leaves the bill. Dave snatches it away before I have time to protest and settles it.

With a grin, he cocks his head.

"Don't worry. Just because I paid doesn't mean it's a date. However, I think you need to reexamine what's going on here."

"And what is it you think is going on?"

Leaning across the table, he lowers his voice.

"I think we enjoy breaking rules together. Giving a big ole fuck you to whoever gives us a hard time. In fact, I think we like it so much we need to work on that part you were thinking of before I found you."

"What part is that?"

He smiles again and I swear, somehow; he makes what should be an innocent smile seem dirty as fuck. Without even saying a word.

"The part where you wanted me to fuck you. Remember? I watched you."

Ah, so it's not an innocent smile after all. My pulse races when I remember what he saw.

"You turned me down."

"I did. But now I know you."

"I don't think you can get to know someone well after a single date."

"Aha! So you *do* think it's a date!"

He points a finger at me in victory.

Dammit. I can't keep my lips from smiling.

"Okay. It felt like a date. You're right. But for the record, I'm really messed up, Dave. I don't know where this will take us. Especially if you're only here for a week."

"Well, you wanted sex, didn't you? And casual. Let's just do that until I have to go."

My heart pounds just thinking of having him whenever I want and I ignore that voice in my brain telling me it's a bad idea. But he's right. It is part of what I want.

Sex. Booze. Maryjane.

I can do it all for a week and get it out of my system. When Dave leaves, I'll detox and try to figure out how to be a valuable member of society again. It's not likely the best idea I've ever had. But it's probably going to be the most fun one.

"Then let's get out of here. The clock is ticking."

Dave might have knocked over his water glass in his hurry to leave the table.

He bumps my shoulder as we speed walk to my Escalade. My head spins with everything that's happened in the last few hours. It's all so fast, but it seems right. He's genuine. I see it in his eyes. But he's also a demon. If he wanted to cause harm, he would have already. Nothing he's done has made me feel unsafe. Quite the opposite.

I don't know how I know he won't harm me. It's no single thing I can name. I just know. And if all demons are like him, I've been misled. But he's also an anomaly, he said. I don't know how I can teach him to be bad, but I'll do my best. Starting with having him use my body anyway he wants.

That's the bad I don't mind being good at.

So caught up in my indecent thoughts, I round the side of my Escalade, too late noticing the men waiting for me between the vehicles.

"We couldn't help but notice your vehicle. My friend and I were commenting it looks like yer moving. That's a lot of boxes in the back. Do ya need any help?"

They both step closer to me and the scrape of a knife blade popping open has the hair on my neck stand.

Faking a smile, I place my hand on the door handle.

"Oh, I'm not staying in town or I'd take the help. That's kind of you to ask."

The one closer to me with the knife lunges and twists my arm behind my back.

"Just give us yer wallet and keys and I won't leave ya here bleedin' out."

"Let him go."

In my panic, I'd forgotten I wasn't alone. Dave steps within distance of the man with the knife.

"This don't concern you, man. We just want the money and the car."

"Don't make me ask you twice."

The tip of the knife presses with more force against my side and the burger I enjoyed threatens to make a return appearance.

"Not another step or he gets it."

Dave sighs like it's the biggest inconvenience and what happens next will be seared into my brain forever. Dave's hand flies out, yanking the man off me with the ease of a child tearing tissue paper. His eyes burn red. Two molten balls of fire that don't even resemble eyes, as he tosses the man aside before turning his attention to the second threat.

"What the fuck are you?"

The second carjacker stumbles and falls on his ass in his haste to put distance between him and Dave. But Dave isn't having it. He picks him up by the throat and drags him to where his friend still lies, moaning on the ground.

"I'm your worst nightmare. And you picked the wrong person to fuck with today. Nobody threatens what's mine."

Tossing the man to the ground with his friend. Dave doesn't look back. Instead, he strides toward me. Jaw set, he runs his hands over my body. "Are you hurt?"

Shaking my head, I push him away and vomit on the pavement before slumping against the SUV.

Voices of others penetrate through my fog as I'm carried to the passenger side. He settles me in the seat and buckles me in. Brushing the hair away from my forehead, he squeezes my leg before closing the door and rounding the front of the vehicle.

Without another word, he pulls away from the parking lot and the crowd gathering.

And I pass out.

DAVE

The entire drive to Mike's house, Charles remains asleep. He's not unconscious. I think he was initially, but he's been fluttering his eyes and talking in a fitful sleep the entire time.

Fucking carjackers. What would have happened if I wasn't there? He's so kind and naïve and as much as he wants to put on that tough mask, I know he's not. He's just as soft as me, and this arrangement will not go as planned. I'm not willing to walk away either. Handbook and rules be damned.

Charles needs someone in his corner. I don't mind it being me.

When he finally opens his eyes, we're parked in a carport next to what I assume is Mike's house.

He groans as he wiggles and sits up.

"I hope they have a bathroom here. I need to piss."

"We have to wait for Mike before we go in."

He's silent for a few minutes, leaning his head against the window.

"Did you break another demon rule at the Burger Barn?"

Oh, I'm sure there were a few I broke.

"If I did?"

"Is it my fault?"

"You weren't paying attention. My actions aren't your fault."

"You went easy on them. For me. I feel like that's my fault."

He's right. I went easy, but I also didn't want to subject him to anything gory. He was clearly not ready to handle what I really was capable of. I didn't want him to witness Dave, the demon. I selfishly wanted him to see Dave, his rescuer, and a nice guy.

"The only person at fault is me, Charles. I'm not good at being bad, remember? I never have been. You were in trouble. I couldn't stand there and watch you get hurt."

"Thank you."

His voice is raspy and if I didn't know better, I'd think no one has ever stood up for Charles before. He's been everyone's doormat. And that makes me... sad.

I hate that he thinks my transgressions are his fault.

"Before all that went down, you mentioned you wanted to just be yourself and have people see you for Charles and not the guy at the front of the church. I guess we're sort of the same that way, you and me."

Charles lets his shoulders sag, and he shifts in his seat towards me.

"Yeah, maybe we are."

"How come you became a priest if you hate it so much?"

Charles picks at invisible lint on his pants.

"I never used to hate it." His voice is so broken. So hurt. "I loved being the one people came to for advice and help, but it wasn't my first choice." He twiddles his thumbs together and shifts his face to look out the window. "My foster parents didn't accept me as I was. They were very conservative and disapproved of... of me. I so desperately wanted their love. I tried to be something I wasn't." His throat clicks with a heavy swallow. "The insistence I keep my sexual preferences a secret made me follow this path. They were such staunch catholics I felt if I was a priest, someone in the church that was respected, maybe they would still love me."

Charles looks down at his fidgeting fingers and I've never wanted to hug someone more than I do now.

"Do you still speak to them?"

"No. A few years ago, I told them I wasn't happy, and I'd always be gay. I thought about leaving the church before I was involved with Matthew. They hadn't changed their minds. I'm dead to them."

He snorts a kind of sad sound and tries to smile.

"So I may as well keep on going on, right? I have nobody waiting for me. It's just me."

Before I have a chance to say any words of comfort, a knock on the driver's side window has both of us yelp.

A man with short brown hair speaks, and his voice is muffled through the window.

"Dave? I'm Mike."

Exiting the vehicle, we meet Mike between the vehicle and the house. He wears several leather bracelets on both wrists and has a messenger bag slung across his body. The bags under his eyes concern me. He seems like a guy carrying a lot of weight on his shoulders.

"What is it I can help you both with?"

"Well, my dad said to contact you. We need a place to stay."

I tower over Mike. Mike doesn't even reach my shoulders and seems completely unaffected by what I am. Of course if he knows my dad, he's aware I'm a demon.

"Right, so about that. I have a place, but you're not alone."

"Okay. That's fine. Is the vehicle okay out here?"

"Oh, yeah. That's not a problem. Grab your stuff and I'll show you around. The others should be home."

I grab the small bag I know Charles packed from the back of the Escalade and with a hand on his back, we follow Mike into the house.

"I'll need to borrow some of your clothes. I didn't get to pack anything before I left." I whisper next to his ear, and I'm thrilled to see him shiver.

"We're not exactly the same size."

"I'll just stay naked then and borrow your toothbrush."

Charles sucks in a breath. "You won't hear me complain."

Mike casts a glance back at us as he opens the door. "Did your dad tell you about my place at all?"

I slip back into serious mode and notice Charles adjust his crotch as Mike steps inside.

"No. Just that you owed him and it wouldn't be a problem."

The house is massive, reminiscent of sprawling farm houses when settlers came here and had a dozen children just to work the land. It's old and has many additions. I easily noticed the additions with the change in building materials and style. It's a unique home in the way it blends architectural styles across two hundred years. Like it kept trying to adapt to the changes in society without saying goodbye to its structural roots.

A young man with long dark hair moves around the kitchen, swinging his hips to music only he hears since he's wearing headphones. Mike taps him on the shoulder and he spins towards us.

"This here is Xavier. We call him Cook sometimes though, because that's what he does best."

I extend a hand in greeting, but he ignores it, scanning Charles before turning to Mike.

"He's human. I thought you said we couldn't do that unless we knew they were... chosen."

Before Mike can say anything, I step closer, growling loud enough to make the young man take a step back. "He's with me. I chose him, and that's all you need to know."

Xavier holds up his hands. "Sorry. I should have waited. Not a problem. Down, boy. I get the message. Welcome. Like, Mike said, call me Cook or X. I'm really only good at cooking, I make a terrible witch. That's why you find me here most of the time."

This time he shakes my hand and I make sure he notices

the flames in my eyes as he casts another appreciative glance at Charles. Witch or not, he can stay away.

Mike motions for us to follow him down a long hallway that ends in a massive oak door.

"This is a suite you're welcome to as long as you like. There's a key on top of the dresser, but you shouldn't need to lock anything here. If you don't mind, I've had a very long day and I need some sleep. We can catch up in the morning if that's okay?"

"Of course. I think we'll be okay now that we're here. Nothing is urgent for us. Thank you, Mike."

With a nod, Mike opens the door and... vanishes.

"Did he just disappear or I am still high from last night's joint? Dave?" His voice rises with a squeak. "What the hell is this place?"

Charles shakily lowers himself to the king size bed, noticing the satin bedding as I do. But the satin doesn't hold his attention very long as he clenches his fists on his thighs.

"Charles? Do you need something?"

A panic laden laugh leaves his lips.

"I need to feel like I'm in touch with reality again. I just left the only life I've ever known. I was almost car jacked and I'm sitting in a strange house with a witch, a disappearing man and a demon who is extra nice. This isn't real. I need.... I need to..."

He pulls in deep breaths; the panic gripping him as he lowers his head to his knees. "I need you to help me understand how the hell I'm here talking to someone who was a figment of my over sexualized imagination twenty four hours ago and how any of this is happening. Help me stop freaking out."

I was wondering if any of this would make him crack. As a priest, it's not that big of a stretch for him to believe I'm real. But the rest of it, yeah, any human would likely panic. Or be on the cusp of a melt down as Charles seems to be.

I toss my suit jacket over the back of the chair before sitting next to him and pulling him onto my lap. He feels so tiny against me, but he also melts into my chest, clutching me like a lifeline and a peace I've never felt before settles. I dust my lips across his forehead.

"It's a lot to absorb for you. I'm sorry I dragged you into it."

"Stop apologizing. You saved my life. If you weren't there, I'm sure I'd no longer be breathing."

My heart aches imagining that kind of outcome for him.

"But would you have been there in the first place? I know you had no plan, but would you have gone there if you were alone?"

"I don't really know. Probably? I thought... fuck, I just wanted to go somewhere and lose myself in sex and alcohol, to be honest. It was the only thing to numb the pain of Matthew that worked."

I knew I should have done something to that guy instead of escorting him out of the building. It's his fault Charles is so bruised.

"Humans lose themselves in indulgence. You're no different from anyone else that way. You have strong emotions to cope with. I'm not one to judge. But I'll help you however you need me to."

His hand smacks my chest, but there's no animosity behind it.

"You're not here to help me. You should be out doing less than kind things if you want to redeem yourself and return home. I can't teach you that. I only know how to be unkind to myself."

I didn't think it was possible for me to feel so strongly towards anyone, let alone a human, but those words tear at my heart like a rusty saw blade. Dammit, I'm not making it out of here in one piece.

"Charles?"

"Yeah?"

"Do you want me to make you forget all that? Do you want me to make your body sing so loud you fall asleep without all that stuff clogging your mind for a night?"

"You want to blow my mind?"

"Oh, I'll blow more than your mind. Yes or no, Charles?"

I know this isn't healthy, but I don't care. If he wants to use sex to forget the pain he has and if it helps even for a minute, I'll do that. It helps me forget my own problems too, that's sort of selfish isn't it?

"Yes. Make me forget it all. Just make me feel... something else."

His arms squeeze me tighter before I stand, taking him with me in my arms. He wraps his arms around my neck as I turn and bend to lay him gently on the bed.

"Can I call you Chuck?"

A laugh slips out of his lips and he tracks my fingers as I unbutton my shirt.

"Uh, sure."

"Charles is so formal. Chuck is like... laid back. Fun. Sexy."

I toss my shirt with my suit jacket on the chair and kneel over him. His eyes rake over me and I know he likes what he sees. If I can be guilty of anything, it's vanity. I know I look good and it's always a boost when another man appreciates it.

"I've never been accused of being fun. Or sexy."

"Really? They need glasses and to check their personalities. You're both."

My horns emerge and with a tentative hand, he reaches out to run his fingers over them.

"Does that hurt? When they go up and down like that? Do you have any kind of control over it?"

The breathless wonder in his voice makes my heart soar.

"It doesn't hurt and I can usually control it. Sometimes, though, I can't. Like now. When I'm aroused and want something, they grow fast. Not much different from an erection, I'm afraid."

I dip my head for him to have a closer look, and he rubs a fingertip up and down one of my horns. It grows before his eyes and I purr with appreciation. Nobody ever wants to love on the horns. They scare people. But I love having them touched. Especially the way Charles is.

"Do you want me that much?"

"Like my next breath."

"Then take it. Make me forget."

CHARLES

Prior to today, I didn't know I'd have a fetish for demon horns. But here I am, stroking the ones on Dave's head and rejoicing as they keep growing.

And when I tell him to take me, the growl from deep in his chest sends a wave of lust so strong through my body, I fear I'll come as soon as he touches me. Matthew never looked at me the way Dave is now and for the first time, I feel like I'm wanted for me and not just because I'm convenient.

After weeks of being an asshole and indulging in everything ever denied me, the admission that I was running from the pain of a broken heart is shocking even to me. I knew I was hurting, but that's a truth I never wanted to admit. That Matthew had that kind of hold on me to send me into such a spiral was safer if I just ignored it.

I'm told the best way to get over someone is to get under someone else. Or I read it. Either way, at this moment, it's a solid plan.

Dave's hands are warm, bordering on hot, and as he smooths them under my shirt to pull it off, I gasp when his palms linger on my sensitive nipples.

"Shit. It feels like you laid a hot pack on my entire body."

"Oh, I should have warned you. Are you too hot? When I'm turned on, I uh, heat up."

Ah, fuck, that bashful smile is everything.

"No, I'm fine. Fantastic actually."

He pauses and in his blue eyes, a flicker dances before he lowers his lips to my exposed skin.

"Ohmymotherofgod."

Dave's lips are possessed. They have to be. Every kiss and every nip or lick against me sends little bursts of pleasure through my entire body. It's like a million tiny lightning bolts.

His lips curve against my skin in a smile as he makes quick work of the zipper of my pants.

"Still no god here, Chuck. Just you and me."

His throaty chuckle mixes with my laboured breathing as he palms my cock through my briefs.

"You're always ready for it, aren't you, Chuck?"

"It seems that way doesn't it? Maybe it's just you."

Sliding the rest of my clothes off, my cock lays heavy against my stomach and he sits back to stare at my complete nakedness.

"If you hadn't imagined me the other night, I probably would have found you on my own, you know. You're beautiful and insatiable. A heady combination for a guy like me."

Swallowing, I bite my lip as he stands and sheds the rest of his clothes. He looks even better than the first time I saw him naked. But this time those giant horns on his head are bigger and his cock... well, there's no way that's going in me. I struggled to get it in my mouth. My ass isn't ready for that. At least, not right now.

"I told you not to worry, Chuck. I won't hurt you and you're right. Your ass isn't ready for it."

"This whole reading my mind thing is creepy and a little unfair."

Dave laughs again and I smile as he lowers himself next to me.

"It's not my fault. Sometimes it happens and sometimes it doesn't. But let's talk about that later. Right now, just know, I'm here for your pleasure. You want me to help you forget, then that's what I'll do."

"It's hard to forget everything when you have horns in my face."

"Fair. But Chuck? Can you touch them like you did before? Don't be afraid of them."

"I'm not afraid, Dave. Quite the opposite."

With the heel of my palm, I slide across the smooth surface. It's cool to the touch and like a piece of river stone. Dave's purr of pleasure makes my dick jump. It must be a direct line to his cock because each time I stroke his horn, he ruts against me.

"Stop."

He whispers before bringing his mouth to mine in a fiery kiss. "This is about you. I like that too much."

Shifting again, he smacks my ass, and the warm chuckle

from earlier is replaced with a wicked tone.

"On your hands and knees, Chuck." He draws out the k with a laugh.

In my want for him to get me off, I do as I'm told. Immediately.

Those too warm hands knead and pull at my cheeks and I groan with the sensation of his hot breath over my skin.

My entire body trembles and I squeeze my eyes shut. I know what's coming and I'm about to start to beg for it if he doesn't hurry. He must read my mind again, because he finally ends my suffering and buries his face between my cheeks.

Does his tongue grow like his horns? It's like the whole thing is everywhere at once and filling me up at the same time. He pins me in place and doesn't let up as I try to wriggle and writhe both away from him and to get closer. My cock is so hard it's downright painful and I'm surfing the edge of the biggest orgasm of my life.

"Let me fucking come already." I moan and collapse on my face since he has my hips in a death grip and I have no other choice.

The loss of his tongue from my ass draws a frustrated cry, but his mouth is underneath me seconds later as he positions me over his mouth again, this time engulfing my whole cock in a single swallow.

My voice freezes. Stuck in my throat because I can't work my mouth to form words and my tongue is lax. My brain is offline. It's all too damn good and in seconds I'm shooting down his throat with no warning.

Like an animal, I can't stop and I'm thrusting myself forward into his mouth as he struggles to swallow everything. Cum trickles out the corners of his mouth and I can't tear my gaze away from his. He's just as gone as I am.

Reaching down, I grip one horn tightly and he gasps around my semi hard cock and juts his hips off the bed. Grinning at him, I shift my balance to both knees and pull his horns in long strokes, one in each hand. It's like a tandem jerk off and oddly erotic as his eyes roll back in his head.

"Chuck..." His pants come faster and god I wish I could take his dick right now. Instead, I shimmy down so I can keep one hand on a horn, one on his dick. That seems to be the magic combination and I don't get far before he's spilling over my fist and reaching for me, dragging me up to his lips, still covered in my cum.

I've never shared such a dirty kiss and yet... It's perfect. And my head spins again, trying to wrap my head around what just happened between us and what this all means. And is this my life now?

Dave rubs his nose next to mine.

"It will be clear in the morning, Chuck. Don't let all the confusing stuff take away from what we just shared."

Those flickering eyes bore into mine again.

"What is it we just shared?"

He takes a longer time to answer me as he gazes at me with something I can't quite put a name to.

"Our souls."

The moonlight comes through the window, bathing our bed in an ethereal glow. Dave snores softly with an arm draped over my hip and his feet tangled in mine.

After we cleaned up from the most mind blowing sex I've ever had, not that I have a lot to compare it to, but it was definitely unexpected. We both drifted off into a deep sleep, comfortably tangled up in each other.

I untangle myself from his grip and after rummaging through my pants pockets; I find what I want and slip out onto the small patio off our room. The moon provides enough light for me to find a lounge chair, and I make myself comfortable before sparking the lighter. Once the joint is lit, I settle back in the chair, content to have the cool evening air wash over my naked skin.

Nude moon bathing with a joint. If I had a bottle of gin, it would be perfect. But no sooner than the thought crosses my mind, it feels wrong. And for the first time since I started breaking my vows to the church, I feel guilty. The number one reason for leaving the way I did was I couldn't hide myself anymore. I wanted to still do good and follow the principles of the bible because it's still filled with valuable lessons, but I was tired of being so handcuffed and forced into a box.

This new found freedom to me has been exhilarating and terrifying. I've not just walked away. I've run naked and barefoot while throwing the bird over my shoulder. There's no going back and I need to work out what it is I need or want next.

Leaning back, I stare at the moon as I puff out the smoke and let the fuzziest of buzzes settle into me. I'd never be able to do this at the rectory.

"Smells like someone sprung for the good stuff."

A figure steps out of the shadows near the wall.

"X was it?" I puff the smoke again in his direction and he nods, stepping closer and pulling up the other chair.

"Yep. I don't think you told me your name, though."

After another drag, I pass the joint to him since he clearly wants it.

"Charles. Do you always roam around here in the dark?"

He laughs before passing the joint back.

"Do you always lie around naked in common areas?"

I can't keep the laugh inside that bubbles out.

"I can't say it's a habit. I didn't think there was anyone awake or out here this time of night, though."

"I don't sleep much so you'll always find me out here. Anywhere really." I feel his gaze heavy on me and even in the dim light of the moon, he's checking me out. He licks his lips when he notices I've caught him looking. "Especially if you lay out here like this all the time."

Our gazes lock, and he's a good-looking guy. His shaggy brown hair and lush lips with all his silver rings give him a low key bad boy vibe.

"And what if I do?"

Handing the joint back to him, he takes a drag and leans in closer, slowly blowing the smoke into my face.

"I might ask you if you want company. I might ask to share the seat with you."

Swallowing, I notice his hair flutters like it's in a breeze, but the night air is calm. He reaches out to run his fingers down my cheek and I'm frozen in place. I'm torn in so many directions right now and my fuzzy brain isn't sure what way is up right now.

As I'm about to answer, Dave's voice booms in the night's silence.

"Get your hands off him. Now."

X doesn't even flinch. He simply takes his hand back and looks between me and Dave.

"Damn. I was hoping I was wrong about you two. Can't blame me for trying." He stands with a step closer to Dave. "Thanks for the... view."

Dave growls and the red flash in his eyes as he stares down X has all my blood rush south.

As X disappears back wherever he came from, I hold the joint in invitation to Dave. He shakes his head. "Why are you out here naked?"

"I couldn't sleep."

"You should have woken me up."

"Then we'd both be awake."

"But you'd not be out here naked for anyone to see. You'd be with me. I'm the only one you can show yourself to, Chuck."

Leaning down, I put out the joint on the brick and pretend his words have no effect on me. But I've been thinking about what he said earlier.

"Is that what you meant last night when you said we shared our souls? Did I get tricked into making a deal with you or something?"

"You were a willing partner."

Maybe it's the weed, or maybe it's just him. Heck, maybe it's the fact I'm naked outside at night. Whatever it is, it's messing with my head and possibly my heart. X has disappeared, and it's just the two of us here now.

When he offers a hand to pull me up from the chair, I take it and he pulls me into his still too hot body.

"You're the first person I've been with I want to wake up to." His hands grip my ass and pull me tight to him. He brings his lips to my neck and kisses me gently. My heart pounds against my rib cage when he bites into my shoulder, sucking hard enough to leave a mark. "If I feel that way, then nobody else can see you like this. Please. Don't come out here naked again."

His voice borders on anguish and I don't know how to feel.

I'm all over the map.

"What if you're with me? Is it okay then?"

His hand sneaks down between us and he wraps it around my leaking cock. Sure slides as he strokes me right there in the moonlight. Fuck, it feels good and I push up on my toes into his fist.

"It's okay when I have my hands on you or my lips. It's okay if my cock is shoved down your pretty throat, but never alone, Chuck. Never. Alone."

His lips are on mine and I'm moaning into his mouth as he backs me up against the side of the house. The vinyl siding is cool against my hot skin and Dave ruts against me, his hard dick sliding across mine as his hot breath whispers in my ear.

"I don't have a soul to share, but I have a heart. Whoever I give it to belongs to me, whether they like it or not."

My head bangs against the siding as he pushes me harder into the house and we frot against each other like wild animals. He pulls one of my legs up around his waist and I clutch at his shoulders.

He pulls aways from my neck, breathing in hard puffs, consumed with lust and I go for it, pulling myself up against him and wrapping my legs around his waist. Once again, he grips my ass and slams me back into the house.

"You had no business being celibate. You're too sexy for your own good. One day I'm going to have my dick in you and fuck you against the wall like this."

"Ohmygod... yesss..."

He bites my lip, drawing blood and I yelp, punching my hips forward for more friction, more touch, just more anything.

"I want to come." I breathe as I bury my hands in his hair.

"Use me. Use your hand. Use whatever you want. Do it now, Chuck."

Squeezing myself against him as tight as I can, he thrusts against me and bites down on my neck again.

With a strangled moan, I come between us, and Dave gasps against my skin. He quickly spins and lowers me to the lounger, jacking himself over the top of me.

He comes with a roar I'm sure could wake a hibernating bear, painting me with his cum.

"You'll be the end of me." He rasps.

He pulls me up again, and this time his kisses are more tender.

"Let's get cleaned up again and back to bed. Next time you can't sleep, wake me."

Nodding, I follow him back into the house and I think when his week here is up, he'll be the end of me, too.

DAVE

Who the fuck still drinks instant coffee?

This is not the way to start the day and is a very poor start to what I know will probably be a difficult day. I didn't sleep a wink after Chuck and I went back to bed. He did, though. I have the dried drool on my chest to prove it.

"Who pissed in your cornflakes this morning?"

X's voice breaks through my thoughts and fills the empty kitchen.

"Whoever didn't have the good taste to have real coffee in this kitchen. Do you drink this shit daily?"

He takes in the mess I left on the counter with the spoon, kettle and instant coffee jar and snorts.

"I don't drink it at all. I use it to cook with." He bends down and removes a coffee maker and tin of grounds from a lower cupboard. "We have good stuff right here. You didn't look hard enough."

I want to say something scathing, but he's making real coffee, so I choose to bite my tongue.

"I'm surprised you're awake. After the way you owned

Charles on the patio last night, I figured you'd be in bed until noon. We keep Gatorade in the pantry if you need it."

He sits across from me with a smirk and I count to ten. It wouldn't be wise to smash my coffee cup into his face.

"I hope you enjoyed the show because that's as close as you'll ever get to him."

Waving his hand, a tray of muffins from the counter floats over and drops onto the table with a thump, spilling some muffins out. X curses and cleans up his mess with a fast glance towards me.

"Before you say anything, I already know I need to work on the finishing move. I start strong but can never finish. That's my problem."

"I hope your lovers don't talk like that to you."

His mouth gapes as I move to pour a cup of coffee, real coffee, now that the machine has brewed. Because I've learned, I'll never stop being nice, I also bring a cup over to X.

"I've never had the chance to get that far, so I wouldn't know."

My eyebrows shoot up with that admission. He was coming on to Charles hot and heavy last night and he has no experience? That's... ballsy.

"So, what brought you two here, if I may ask? You didn't even have time to pack."

"How do you know that?"

He gestures to my body.

"Strange house, no shirt and sleep pants that clearly aren't yours. Am I right?"

Delaying the answer while I drink my coffee, I think of how much I should tell him. I don't even know how Mike got here and the deal with my dad yet.

"How long have you been here?"

Deflection for information is the better strategy.

"Almost four years now." He breaks apart a muffin and slides the tray towards me. "They sent me out of my coven because I can't fit in."

"That seems harsh. What's the story?"

He leans back, picking the walnuts out of the carrot muffin and placing them to the side.

"Witches need to cast spells. Not only am I not good at them, but I also don't like to use them for bad things. It makes me feel gross. My family wasn't on the side of white magic." He pauses, and a shadow crosses his face. "Mike found me and told me I could stay here. I've never left."

I watch as he arranges the walnut pieces in a single long row in front of him and eats one from each end.

"Are you happy here? Do you go out into the human world and manage, okay?"

With a playful grin, he snaps his fingers over the walnuts and they form the word yes before bouncing and falling off the table.

I chuckle as he sighs and gathers the pieces off the floor.

"I manage well enough to blend in. Sometimes I forget, though, and I might reach for something high on a shelf and summon it instead. When I do that, it's always a scramble to cover it up. I look like another human being, so there's that, too. It's when we're in private I can't always hide things. Like my witch's mark or how sometimes my auto spells just happen. That's why, I uh, that's why I have no experience."

Clearing his throat, he drinks his coffee and I refill mine. The too small sleep pants of Charles' I found won't do for a week. I'll have to get something else to wear because I'm not sitting around in a suit for five more days. And I should likely remember my manners and not sit at a stranger's table with no shirt on.

"Good morning, gentlemen."

Mike appears next to me, reaching for the coffee pot and a mug. He shifts his glance between X and me.

"Are you two getting along, okay?"

"X was telling me you found him and brought him here. What is this place, Mike?"

Mike settles with a weary sigh at the table with us.

"To put it as simple as possible, it's a place for misfits. Those from other worlds and sometimes humans with special circumstances."

I scrunch my nose at his description. "We're not misfits. I don't like that word at all. There's nothing wrong with us."

"You never told me what brought you here." X nudges me under the table with his foot. "I'm not stupid. I know you were trying to distract me."

Biting my lip, I peer into the cup before me. A mere

forty-eight hours ago, I was in a completely different world. I had a family. I was in a comfortable space. It wasn't a perfect existence, but I thought I belonged there.

Now I'm not so sure I was meant to be there at all.

"How do you know my father, Mike? Let's start with that."

"Sure. So much time has passed. I can't tell you how long ago it's been, but he was there when I needed a miracle." He sips his coffee and a small smile plays at his lips. "It was worth it and I don't regret it."

"So you made a deal with him, then?" I keep my voice soft. Mike's wistful demeanour is noticeable and a glance at X confirms he senses a shift, too.

"My wife was dying. There was no cure. I was working for a farmer at the time doing mainly manual labour. It paid well enough, but it took me away from her. I couldn't bear being away when she had so little time left, but we still had bills to pay." Rubbing at his eyes, it draws my attention to permanent dark circles there. "I got drunk one night after we got the news. It was a pity party. I was so furious. It wasn't fair, you know?"

Swallowing, he huffs out a breath. "We had just moved to this tiny town called Hope. We only wanted a better life, but it got worse." He shakes his head, as if to toss the sad memories away. "Anyway, when I was drunk, I met your father and made a deal. At the time I thought it was just a joke, but right after she died, he showed up at my doorstep."

"Dad is nothing but punctual, especially if souls are involved."

He left family events to collect. Dad was serious about his job.

"Indeed, he was. I said I'd give my soul to just have her a little longer. To see our first Christmas together in this new town. She died two days after Christmas and after her service, I disappeared. He gave me the time and money to be with her for several months and in return, I gave him my service for eternity."

"Wow, you really loved her. That's a hard deal. And I'm sorry for your loss."

Mike toys with his coffee cup as he assesses me.

"Your dad's not as bad as you think, Dave. I know it sounds awful but there are other things at play with my deal with him. And I like to think there's good in it. Besides, I like what I do, mostly."

I'm wondering about how horrible my father really is as well. He's testing me, but I don't know why. I mean, I know why. I'm horrible at being the evil, tyrannical monster I'm supposed to be. My brothers are good at it. Dad is obviously good at it, and yet he's shoved me into the path of Mike. Someone who is in my father's debt for eternity and made a deal for love.

And Mike thinks he's doing a good service. Clearly I'm missing a lot of this story.

"Good morning, everyone. Was there a party, and I wasn't invited?"

Charles shuffles into the kitchen, rubbing sleep from his eyes. His blond hair is a dishevelled mess, and he's wearing a pair of shortcut shorts with a tank top. He might as well wear nothing at all. The shorts barely cover his ass and the top shows a lot of skin. Like a lot.

X hums in appreciation as Charles turns his back to us and helps himself to the coffee pot. I growl and flare my eyes in his direction. X laughs, a knowing smirk in place as I hurry to help Charles.

"Let me get that for you. You should have slept in. You had a long night."

Dipping my mouth closer to his ear, I whisper, "Do you own shorts that maybe cover more of your ass?"

Looking over his shoulder, he nods to both Mike and X.

"You took my sleep pants, and I wasn't about to go commando in a pair of jeans to breakfast."

"Don't let us stop you! Wear anything you like. I know I don't mind." X laughs into his coffee cup, but Mike punches him in the arm.

"Behave. We have things to work out. Don't cause any unnecessary tension."

Mike rises with his cup, placing it in the sink next to us. "Once you two get sorted this morning, find me in my room. X can show you where it is. If you're going to stay here, you'll need to know a few things."

Before either of us can answer, he vanishes.

"I'll never get used to that," Charles says as he stirs sugar into his coffee. "So, X, did you have a good night?"

"Not as good as you, but I sure did."

Charles pauses and glances at me.

"He watched us. Outside."

Charles flushes and looks away. "Uh, sorry about that."

Laughing, X rises and with a wave of his hand, he makes the remaining items on the table reappear on the kitchen counter.

"Don't be. I'm going to put dinner on in the slow cooker. You two can go about your business."

I motion for Charles to follow me to the sitting room off the kitchen, and we settle onto a love seat near the largest stone fireplace ever created. Once seated, I wiggle and stretch to scratch a persistent itch on my back.

"Can you scratch my back? I just can't get the right spot and it's been irritating me all morning."

Charles sets his cup down, and with both hands, he chases after the itch. It feels good but yet never quite goes away.

"Maybe it's the soap from the shower and you have sensitive skin?"

"Could be. I'm sensitive apparently, so might as well have sensitive skin to match."

There's a heavy silence sitting with us and Charles fiddles with the hem of his shirt. My back still itches but I ignore it, focusing on Charles, and with a finger I tilt his chin towards me. His green eyes are stormy, like he has his own internal battle going on, just like I do.

"Before we go see Mike, I need to say something."

He nods, licking his lips, and my gaze focuses on how they shine with saliva.

"I laid awake last night after we fucked on the patio. There were a lot of things I had to sort. One of them was why I was claiming you when I knew I only had seven days."

"Five now," he whispers.

"Right. Five more days of casual sex for you because you're discovering all these things about yourself. Five more days of me hoping you drink less and don't smoke too much because it lowers your inhibitions. Five more days of me having to watch other men hit on you. Five more days of me not knowing…" I pause, licking my suddenly dry lips. "Of me knowing I only have days and not years."

"Dave, I… I don't even know what's happening to me. I woke up because I had sex with someone who grows horns and I liked it. I loved being naked outside!" He laughs and pulls his head back, gazing down at his trembling fingers. "I felt guilty for the first time last night that I.. that I broke my vows to be this person who wallows in whatever debasing acts possible. I felt free, but I also felt trapped. Because I can't go back, Dave. And you'll be gone in five days. I can't move forward past your time with me. I don't know what I'm supposed to do now."

When he raises his eyes to mine, I can't meet them.

Because I don't know what to do either.

The handbook mentions nothing about what happens if you're the one choosing not to return.

Charles

Mike's room is a suite, much like the one Dave and I are sharing. A bed to one side with a sitting area on the other and a large ensuite with a walk-in closet. The door was open, and he called for us to enter after Dave lightly tapped on the door.

After our conversation in the sitting room, neither of us knew what we should say and instead of trying to work out what it all meant for us, we wordlessly agreed to get over to Mike's room instead.

"So, Mike, I'm thankful for your hospitality, but if me being here is an issue, I can leave. X mentioned humans aren't welcome when we arrived and I don't want to upset anything."

Mike leans forward, elbows on his knees, and sighs.

"You're not upsetting anything. I was actually expecting you. Well, not you exactly, but I knew someone like you would be here."

Dave's knee presses into mine and he wiggles around. Knowing he's likely still itchy, I rub my hand on his back and make a note to find him some oatmeal lotion later when I'm out.

Mike walks over and closes the door before sitting with us again.

"X doesn't need to know about this conversation. He has enough worries. Dave, I know why your dad sent you to me."

"Okay, and are you to help me decipher this useless handbook so I can go back?"

Mike pauses, assessing Dave carefully.

"I'm not, nor have I ever, been a being from a different realm. I'm still considered a human in the very simplest of terms. I have a gift, for lack of a better word, that I didn't fully tap into when I was alive. But... it's important for you both to know my gift is helping others transition."

Dave stiffens at Mike's words.

"Transition how?" I ask. Because all of this makes little sense to me. Dave doesn't want to stay here. He wants to go back to the underworld. At least I'm pretty sure he does.

"To their new life. Whether it be in a new town, a new world, or guiding a soul to where they should be. Dave, your dad thinks I can help you."

Dave shoots off the couch and paces the length of the room. He's still wearing my sleep pants that barely reach his ankles and cling to his muscles like a second skin. If the situation we're in wasn't so surreal, I'd probably laugh.

"Are you saying he doesn't want me to try? He doesn't want me back there?"

"I think he wants you to experience a different way of living and let you judge."

Dave shakes his head, pressing his lips together.

"No. This doesn't make sense. Why wouldn't he just incinerate me on the spot if he wanted me gone? I know I've brought disgrace to him with my too tender ways but I was going to try! I thought you would help me try..." His voice trails off with a gulp. "I thought you'd help me try to do what he wants."

Mike is a hard one to read. His face remains blank and gives nothing away.

"Someone rescued your father once. Did you know that? If it wasn't for that single moment, he would have died hundreds of years ago. He'd certainly not be where he is now."

Dave's brow scrunches in confusion. "His father appointed him. He earned the space through birth order and trials of suffering. He's revered in the underworld as the hardest demon to bargain with. He's... he's every demon's hero. So I don't know what you mean."

"You should sit, Dave. Please."

He doesn't want to. Dave is wound tight and the room's temperature spikes with his anxiety. But he settles next to me and surprises me by taking hold of my hand in a tight squeeze.

"Tell me."

Mike leans forward again and his calm demeanour leaves me to believe nothing would ever phase this guy. Not if he's been through all these weird things he says he has.

"Just before you were born. Your dad got himself into a right pickle of a situation. He was cocky and arrogant and if it wasn't for someone stepping in, he'd not be where he is today. Did you find it odd he told you to spend a week on earth and sent you to a church?"

"A little. I thought it was a big test since I'm not exactly known for staying out of trouble. And maybe a little mean, if I'm being honest."

Mike chuckles.

"Faustus has history with a church and it almost killed him. Instead of being drowned in holy water, which was exactly about to happen once the people figured out he was a creature from hell, a woman stood up for him. Saved his life."

Dave's hand squeezes mine tighter. How interesting this all is to me, but Dave is confused. Growing more angry with each word from Mike. I've only seen what Dave does when angry and protecting me. What would he do if he's angry with someone who dared lie to him?

"A woman in a church saved my dad? A single woman? How?"

Mike seems hesitant to tell the rest of the story, but neither of us will leave until it's finished.

"Tell us how a single woman accomplished this and what the hell does it have to do with Dave being here?"

"The woman was sweet on Faustus. He had charmed her already. She was hoping to turn him to her side, but he wasn't having it. Yet she still saved him. Dave... it was your mother who got him out of there by appealing to the people threatening him. He was simply a man gone off course and they should show him mercy and forgiveness."

"Like we teach them, too. Do unto others as you would have done to you." I whisper, and Dave's face pales.

"My mother died during childbirth. I never knew her."

Mike stands and removes a book off a shelf nearby. Flipping it open to a page, he hands the book to Dave.

"There were seven angels sent to earth to walk among us and protect us from the evil that was seeping through from hell. Guardians, if you will. Your mother was one of them."

Silence so thick it's hard to breathe settles in the room. Dave's eyes scan the pages of the book as his fingers dust over the images.

"My mother was an angel?"

"She was. And I think your dad needs to tell you the rest of the story."

"How do I fit into this? Because I was a man of the church? How did you know I'd be here with him?"

Dave still stares at the photos on the page, unblinking.

Mike nods. "I knew whenever Faustus sent me his son it would be because it was time to tell him all this. And if it was time to do that, he'd want someone with him when he learned the truth who could help him process. Faustus made his own deal, you see. Well, a promise, really. And it was to Dave's mother. Just like I would do anything for my wife, Faustus will honour Dave's mother's wish."

"I need to get out of here."

Dave bolts for the door, leaving the book behind. I move to follow but Mike asks me to stay.

"Let him be alone for a bit. He'll come back to you."

"Mike, I still don't understand. Why me?"

He shrugs. "Because you're a lost sheep too, aren't you? And you're connected to his mom through the church. Not intimately, but in a way that you may be able to explain some things to Dave. Faustus knows what he's doing. I guarantee it."

"Well, it would be nice if he could let us in on what he expects." I glance out the door again. "I don't like him alone. I'm going to find him."

"Of course, I understand. I know how it feels to want to be with the one you love when they're hurting."

"What? I don't love him. I barely know him. I just don't want him to be alone. If I can help, I will."

Mike nods, clearly not convinced by my words.

"You can help. You already have. I'll be away for a few days. If you need anything, talk to X."

I wave over my shoulder with a thanks and rush off to find Dave.

I'm not in love with him. I just can't let him process this kind of news alone. That's what anyone would do. Isn't it?

After returning to our room and finding it empty and Dave not on the patio either, I change into a pair of jeans and return to the kitchen.

X isn't there, but he was. Dishes wash themselves in the sink and a vacuum runs in the sitting room. Although that's probably just a roomba and not magic at work. I think so, anyway.

I don't feel comfortable wandering the huge house on my own since I'm a guest here, and I don't know who else lives here. It seems rude. Now that I'm awake and not stoned, I notice the gorgeous landscaping out back.

Digging through my overnight bag, I find the two items I always carry and, even after the events of the last few months, I still turn to them to comfort me. My rosary and bible. Slipping on my shoes, I make my way across the lawn to a small pond with a waterfall feature. There are several chairs and tables set up bistro style, and the scent of newly blooming roses fills the air.

It's peaceful and just what I need to get a grip on the new information about Dave. And honestly, myself. Part of me would rather find another joint and just let myself drift away into the fuzzy hugs it gives my entire body. Or a few gin and tonics to erase the memory, if I could. But no matter how hard we try, we can't change things about ourselves overnight. Sometimes, it's not possible at all.

After making myself comfortable in one of the chairs, the movement of the rosary beads through my fingers brings me focus and for the first time in a long time, I feel the anxiety slide off me and slither to the nearby pond, leaving me more focused than ever before.

It's okay for me to not want to live the life of a priest and be married to the church. There are too many things I disagree with on a basic level for it to fit right with who I am. There was a time when searching the bible brought me comfort and peace when I was alone. The same passages, some interpreted as being against people like me, people under the rainbow, are also passages I interpret as teaching us to accept and celebrate all our differences.

I may have allowed myself to step off the pedestal of the church, but I can't fully pull myself away from these habits of comfort. The pull to help someone in need has always been my calling.

My mind drifts to Dave, though. I'm confused about the entire situation. I can only imagine how he feels and all I want to do is ease his troubles and mind. Not to mention I still need to find him an anti-itch lotion. And I should also find a better shower soap. Little things make a big difference.

If I can make the difference in even one life, I'm still serving humankind. I'm still considered a good person to do that if he's a demon, aren't I? He's still flesh and blood and, while different from me, he still has a heart. I know because I've felt it beat against my cheek as I drifted off to sleep against him in the most peaceful of sleeps I've had in years.

The wetness on my cheek startles me and I wipe away the tears that can't stop now that they've started. So I pray. Because it's still the only way I know how to soothe my soul. It's all I have left of the person I used to be. The one who always tried to do right for others.

I hope Mike is right that Dave needs me to help him.

Because Mike *was* right.

I think I'm in love with Dave.

Dave

After I left Mike and Charles behind, I had to get out of the house. I needed space to process all this unexpected information. I didn't even bother with shoes and I'm still wearing the ridiculously small pants of Charles'.

Chuck.

I noticed the horrified look on his face when Mike said my mother was an angel. Fuck, I probably had the same look on mine. Followed quickly by anger towards my dad for never telling me. How could he have kept that a secret all these years?

I couldn't sit there any longer. After pacing our room for a few minutes, I left through the patio door out onto the grounds. I found a small pond near the back of the property and there was a cluster of wild rose bushes and raspberry canes behind the perfectly manicured shrubs. It was exactly what I needed.

Without pause, I walk into the untamed prickly plants and let the thorns scrape and poke me. It's not an extreme torture by any means, but it works to draw blood. A reminder that I'm alive and I'm not just a being who's lost his identity. I can focus on the stinging from the scrapes and thorns rather than the tornado of confusion in my head. For a long time, I sit on the grass watching the tiny rivulets of blood run down my chest and arms. It wasn't the pain of welts from a lashing, but the stinging of the shallow cuts was enough for me to focus on who or what I was.

And I wasn't sure now.

I've spent my entire life trying to be the horrible demon my father was hoping for. I tried to make my dad proud and be like my brothers. It was always hard. There was never a day it was easy to be, well, to be cruel. When the last man had the adorable pet rabbit, I knew it would land me in hot water, but I couldn't help it.

Has it been this hard all these years because I wasn't a full demon? Was I just more like my angelic mother and no matter how hard I tried, it wouldn't ever be enough?

So many questions and not nearly enough answers.

And what about Charles? Sure, he was already leaving the church in spectacular fashion, not that I'm complaining. The man can suck a dick like nobody's business and that's a gift he needs to share. Well, not with everyone, just me. *Only* me. And when I allow the word *forever* to float through my thoughts, I don't know if it will happen.

Or how?

And that thought makes me feel... lost.

When I feel like I've sat alone, bleeding and feeling sorry for myself long enough, I make my way back to the pond. And I see him there.

My Charles.

And the wetness on his cheeks has my heart pounding out of control. Without a second thought, I walk right up to him and startle him with my words.

"Why are you crying, Chuck?"

He gasps and drops the rosary before standing and touching his fingertips to my scratched and bleeding chest.

"What happened to you, Dave?"

My tongue can't form words to reply. I only grip his wrist, bringing his fingers to my mouth and kissing each one. The flush in his cheeks fans the fire in my belly for this tender, yet extremely passionate man.

Even I know he's thrown himself into drugs, alcohol, and excessive sex to escape the tangles of his conscience. I've never wanted to save anyone so badly in my life.

Will he stay with me if I can't go back? Is he really here to steer me to what I was perhaps born to do?

This man who has spent his entire life pretending to be someone he isn't sure has a lot in common with me. Only I wasn't pretending. I really didn't know the common thread that binds us together.

My gaze lands on the rosary and bible nearby before returning to his handsome face. This isn't a time for me to be angelic.

"If you want to make me feel better, you can open your pretty mouth for me."

I know he'll say yes and since it's his way to cope with our conflicted paths, I'll make it mine, too. Especially since our future is so foggy.

The tremble in his body sends a new rush of blood to my cock.

"I think I'd do anything for you," he whispers.

He unzips his jeans, freeing his already weeping dick before dropping to his knees in front of me and offering me his mouth.

Without waiting, I clench a fistful of hair and shove my cock in his mouth. He chokes with the sudden intrusion, but not for long. He's already stroking his own erection mercilessly while I abuse his throat. He's so perfect.

"You're so good at this, Chuck. You love having dick in your mouth, don't you?"

He tries to nod but my hand holds him in place and he moans around my cock instead.

"Such a dirty boy. You don't even care if we have an audience again, do you?"

Again, he tries to shake his head and I hold his head tight, burying his nose into my curls. His hand on his own dick never stops moving, even when I know he likely can't breathe.

"Come for me. If you come, I'll let you breathe."

That's the switch he needed. His body jerks and he spurts onto my feet. I pull out of his mouth and he sucks in a lungful of air, all while gazing up at me. Waiting for me to finish. His lips are so puffy and red. Lines of drool string from his lips to my cock.

Maybe I am a devil to wish for him like this anytime I want.

"Mark me," he rasps. "Please."

He couldn't have picked more perfect words. With a groan, I shoot cum all over his pretty face. It's in his hair, down his neck and his blissed-out face has me drop to my knees in front of him.

"Will you stay and help me, Chuck?"

My voice cracks with the question because I can't bear to hear him answer anything other than *yes*.

"Yes. I told you, I'll do whatever you ask."

His voice is raspy from my abuse to his throat, and I wipe the mess off his cheeks.

"Why?"

"Because you need me."

We say no more as I help him to his feet and we walk back to the house, completely and utterly wrecked. I'm covered in bleeding scratches and he's coated in cum and now missing his shirt.

We still say nothing as we help each other clean up, and he picks a few raspberry thorns from my arms.

It's not until we've found some clean clothes for him and me in my suit with a borrowed pair of underwear that he finally breaks the silence.

"Want to get a taco? I'm starving."

"As long as it's not Taco Bell, you've got a deal."

Demon rule or not, you'll never find me at a Taco Bell.

Charles chose to drive us to a food truck somewhere in the middle of town. I wanted to unpack the Escalade before we went out so as not to draw any unwanted attention again, but Charles insisted we wouldn't a second time. Something about lightning won't strike twice and rather than argue, I nodded in agreement.

The food is amazing and we sit at a picnic table sharing a dish of chips and salsa, sipping our drinks. It's a gorgeous summer day and being out here feels almost normal. Usually I don't relax when I'm on earth, but with Charles I feel at ease. Just having him smile at me while his tongue darts out to lick salsa from the corner of his mouth makes this whole situation feel comfortable. Fated, maybe.

"How did you know this taco truck was here?"

He swallows his chip, and his green eyes glow.

"It was totally random." He gestures with his hands almost smacking over his drink." I was driving home from a conference and took a wrong turn. I found this place and stopped while I got myself turned around and back on course."

"It was a lucky day for you then."

His smile fades some, and he shakes his head. "Not really. That conference wasn't a good one. It was the single event to drive me from the priesthood for good." His previous cheerfulness disappears like the sun behind a storm cloud. "I'd been thinking of leaving by then, but after that weekend it was the push I needed."

Crunching chips and feeling closer to him than anyone ever, I hazard to ask him what happened.

"Will you tell me why?"

Charles puffs a breath and eats another chip smothered in salsa.

"There was a group of us having dinner the first night in the hotel restaurant. Our server was a young man, early twenties, very attractive. He was wearing a few different coloured bracelets. He was utterly charming. Just a lovely person, right?" He pushes the remaining chips to me. "The meal was going well and the server, I think his name was Caleb actually, was just one of those people who made the experience better with his company. Anyway, near the end of dinner, when he asked if we'd like dessert, one of the other priests made a comment on how nice he was and that his girlfriend was one lucky lady."

Charles presses his lips together, meeting my gaze.

"I'm sure you know where this is going."

Nodding slowly, I reach across to take his hand.

"Long story short, Caleb casually said his boyfriend is indeed lucky and would he like a scoop of ice cream with his pie? And Dave... I've never been so disappointed in a single person's actions in my life. The man was someone I trusted and almost came out to because I thought he was good. Like I could trust him with it, right? Because other than Matthew I had no one to talk to. I couldn't tell anyone or risk being a pariah."

Charles chews at his lip, clearly fighting to keep emotions in check and I'm sorry I asked him the question.

"You don't have to explain, Charles. I understand."

"The way he spoke to Caleb after that was so cruel and... I knew I didn't want to be associated with it anymore. The secrets and thinly veiled hatred. I was just done."

He exhales a long breath, regaining his composure.

"You know I never thought I'd say hell is better, but with things like this, there's really no issue. Nobody cares who you choose to get down with. I suppose if I need to find one good thing from my past, it's that I never had to deal with the labels of sexuality that you have. I'm sorry."

Charles slurps the last of his drink with a shrug.

"Humans. Am I right?"

His sunshine smile returns and I'm relieved.

"So, we best get you some clothes for a few days, right? You can't always take my underwear."

He stands to leave and I snatch his wrist before he can walk away.

"Do you mean wear or take? Because I plan to take them as much as possible."

He gulps and before he can reply, an elderly couple asks if we're leaving and he gracefully offers our space before walking to his vehicle. I hurry to gather the trash of our meal and dispose before catching up with him.

"Get in before I get a hard on in front of all these families."

Well, I think I just got my answer.

"You should've warned me you like to shop. You only need a few days of clothes, not a month."

Charles' words shouldn't chaff, but they do.

"I could've come by myself, you know."

I really don't need the reminder about my days left here and we still haven't spoken about the morning's information bomb, either. Which we need to do because I'm ready to make a call no matter what my father said.

Charles shoves all the bags he was carrying at me, and while I juggle all the bags, he tucks the keys to his SUV into my suit coat pocket.

"You can get the bags into the vehicle and I'll meet you there. I'm stopping at the drugstore to get something for your back. I won't be long."

When he notices the scowl on my face, he pats my cheek. "No need to frown. It means you'll get naked for me while I rub you down. Win-win."

Even now, it pulls a smile to my face, and I do as he asks while he ducks into the drugstore in the mall. It's nearing the end of the day and the parking lot is much more empty than when we got here.

I locate the vehicle and jam all the bags into the backseat, shoving a few boxes of Charles' things to the side. I'm grateful he has such a large car but we should have just unpacked these boxes before leaving. Tossing my jacket on the front seat, I pocket the keys and lean against the car while I wait.

Now is as good a time as any. Staring at my phone, I text my dad before I lose the nerve. When the phone vibrates with an incoming call from him immediately my heart drops. Looks like Dad won't let me tiptoe around things.

"Hey, Dad. Thanks for calling."

"Why are you texting before your time is up? I can't help anymore than I have, Dave."

"No, I know that but I, uh, am I able to talk to you in person or is that against rules?"

The pause is another long one, and I hold my breath. I can't drag this out. I need to see him in person.

"I can make something work tomorrow if you'd like."

"Yeah, that would be great. Should I meet you somewhere?"

"I'll come to you."

No goodbye or details, just the flash of a phone on the

screen indicating the call ended and I rest a little easy knowing tomorrow I can talk about my mother and hopefully get answers. But also, I can talk about Charles. He can meet my dad.

The thought sends a little zing through me. My dad meeting the man I love.

Shit.

Do I love him? It could be indigestion, those tacos were spicy.

But the longer I wait for him and think about it, the more I think it's not the tacos.

A sharp image of Charles scared flashes in my mind and I'm on high alert, searching the parking lot for him. Just like when I popped into his brain while he was pleasuring himself, this image is clear, but something's wrong.

Stalking back towards the mall, I keep searching for him and will my heart to stop banging.

A second flash comes, and with a growl, I quicken my steps as I head to the loading dock to the right.

Nobody fucks around with what's *mine.*

Charles

"Gimme the wallet, the whole thing."

"Sure, take it."

I'm pleased my hands stop shaking when I toss the wallet to the man. When he asked if I could help him with his wife, who had fallen, I followed him without question. Focused on my concern to help someone in need, too late, I noticed he lead me to a loading zone and nowhere near parked cars.

But now I notice every small detail. The blood-shot eyes and the reek of sour sweat. The stained clothing and unkempt appearance of someone too far gone to an addiction. It breaks my heart for a fellow human to be pushed to the edge like this.

"What else you got on ya? You look rich. Gimme your shoes."

"I could buy you dinner if you like. I know a place you can stay if needed."

Stepping far too close for my comfort, his surprisingly strong, skinny arm grabs a hold of me. "I can get more than dinner from the crowd I run with, pretty boy." He wipes the back of his hand across his nose. "But I've got other problems and I need cash." His dirty, calloused hand touches my cheek and I don't want to recoil, but I do and it's a mistake.

"Don't you pull away from me! I'm gonna take you around the corner so's nobody can see and if you do what I want, I won't hurt cha. Be a shame to scar your pretty face."

For the first time in my life, my mind is blank. I don't know if I should fight back or how. When I don't move my feet with his pull, he spins and punches me in the face right under the eye. The hot bolt of pain sends tears to my eyes, and briefly, Dave flutters through my thoughts as I try to remain upright.

"Don't fuckin judge me! You don't know what it's like! You fuckin' rich people always think you're better!"

Completely unhinged, he punches me hard in the gut and knocks the wind out of me. When I double over, he comes at me again, but I cover my head with my arms. It's too late to fight back now and I rely on my defences as I cower against the wall. With every punch and kick he lands, I pray I'm lucky he doesn't have a weapon.

And I pray to the god I left behind to forgive me and come to my aid. Because prayer was always my comfort and now, it's the only option left.

The blows stop as suddenly as they started with a muffled thud and grunt from my attacker.

Daring to peek out from under my arms one eye swelling shut, I gasp at what my limited vision takes in.

Dave has my attacker pinned by his throat against the wall. His feet barely touch the ground as he unsuccessfully tries to pry Dave's fingers away.

"I should fucking snap your neck right now and leave you for dead."

Even with my fuzzy vision, I notice the flames of anger in Dave's eyes flare to life, and the man's eyes bulge as he tries to draw in air to speak. Dave releases the chokehold and lowers him, but keeps his hand on his throat.

"What's your issue? Drugs? Booze? What the fuck do you want and you have one chance to answer."

The man wheezes as I push myself to standing.

"I need a fix, man. I can't turn tricks anymore and I need money." He coughs as Dave tightens his grip again.

"Don't hurt him, Dave. Please. It's not his fault."

For several moments, Dave doesn't move. He just holds the man against the wall by his throat. His free hand clenched at his side and his jaw set so tight I fear he might break it.

"Are you okay, Chuck?"

His soft voice contradicts the intimidating posture.

"Yeah, I'm okay. Just gonna be full of bruises and likely a black eye."

A rumbling growl sounds as Dave drops the man completely. He reaches into his pocket and, from his wallet, he pulls a wad of cash and throws it at him.

"Be thankful I didn't kill you. Take that and go. If you ever see this man anywhere near you again, even if it's not your fault, you run the other way. You got me?"

The man stoops down and grabs at the bills.

"Remember my fucking face because if you ever see me again, you better run faster than an Olympic sprinter, because I won't be so nice next time."

My attacker stumbles and lurches out of the little pocket we were in and Dave steps to my side.

"Oh sweetheart, we have to stop meeting like this. How bad is the pain?"

His fingertips dust the side of my swollen face.

"Am I still pretty?" I try to force a laugh, but my gut hurts too much.

Without another word, Dave effortlessly scoops me into his arms to carry me away and I wrap my arms around his neck, never wanting to let go.

"If you sit still, this will go faster."

X fidgets around my head and I flinch away. "You said you were bad with magic. What if you do something and mess me up worse?"

He raises an eyebrow. "Okay, true. But come on, Charles. I won't hurt your face. I like it too much."

Dave elbows him out of the way and takes the bag from his

hand. "You better not have fucked it up, X. I swear if trusting you is a mistake..."

Dave's blue eyes soften as he holds the homemade and apparently magical poultice against my skin. He refused to let me walk into the house when we got here and carried me to our suite. He stripped me of my clothes and found fresh ones in my bag before finally letting me move myself and walk to the kitchen where X said he had a spell to heal the bruises faster.

Dave hovered while X did his thing, and I didn't dare speak. He watched X so closely I would have thought he was the witch and not X. He asked questions and once the concoction was made and wrapped in a towel; I was nervous.

"It's okay, sweetheart. It's not black magic. I watched."

"I trust you."

One hand holds the pack to my face while he curls the other hand behind my neck. His thumb strokes my jaw and I screw my eyes shut.

"I prayed for help," I whisper, afraid to open my eyes. "Then you showed up. You've saved me twice now."

"I guess I have."

"You know you showed mercy both times, right?"

"Yeah, I know."

"Will you be in trouble?"

Daring to open my eyes, Dave still has his soft gaze on me.

"I'll find out tomorrow. Dad's coming."

"Whoa! What? Sir Satan is coming here?" X stumbles against the kitchen chairs and hastily makes a cross over his lips.

"Why did you cross your lips?" I ask.

"Well, I'm hoping it keeps me from saying anything stupid. Lord, just stop my mouth from saying something dumb to the devil, you know?"

"He's not *the* devil!" Dave snaps, and X wisely backs away. "His name is Faustus, and he works for Satan. Very outer circle kind of thing. He's a big deal, but it's not like he goes to Satan's birthday parties or anything."

"Satan has birthday parties?"

Dave glares at X again, who wisely mimes to zip his mouth shut.

"I asked him to come here and not wait the seven days. I think... no, I *need* to know about my mother."

"You sure you're ready?"

Bringing my hand up, I wrap it around his arm that holds the pack to my cheek.

"I'm sure."

He flinches again and reaches for his back.

"I need this itching to stop."

He pulls the poultice away, eyes wide when he glances at X. "Well done. There's barely any bruise or swelling."

"I told you I was good at that. I had enough practice with them on myself."

I don't know if Dave catches it but I notice the cloud that momentarily crosses X's face before he pastes another smile in place. I'll have to see if he needs someone to talk to once all this has died down.

Dave helps me off the counter, and after thanking X again, we return to our suite.

Once the door is closed, he groans more and rubs up on the wall.

"Seriously, Chuck, it's so fucking itchy. I'm happy you got the lotion, but I'm not happy you ran into that guy.""How did you find me, anyway? Was I gone that long?"

He strips off his clothes as I locate the bottle I had stuffed into my coat pocket.

"You probably weren't, but I saw you again. You were in my head, just like when I saw you while you were… taking care of yourself." His lips tilt into a wicked grin but it disappears as fast as it came. "But this time you were crying for help and I knew you were in trouble."

"My prayer," I whisper. "You heard it."

Pausing his undressing, he stares at me for a long time.

"You're on my channel. I told you there's something about you I pick up." He taps the side of his head with a finger. "You're in my head a lot."

He continues to strip and I can't look away. Dave is fit, no six-pack or anything, but you can tell he has muscles. And he's so strong. Like a tiger, real power ripples beneath the surface. I've seen him use that power on people to protect me. I'm not even afraid for my safety. Even seeing his strength up close and the flames that ignite in his eyes when provoked, I'm not concerned he'd ever harm me.

I only have to put lotion on his back to ease his persistent itch, yet he's stripped down completely and stands before me with his thick cock laying heavy against his thigh.

"I thought I should get completely naked ahead of time. I hear rub downs sometimes have happy endings."

I bark a laugh at his unexpected, funny side and step forward to smooth a hand up his chest.

"Or is it a happy new beginning? I don't like endings, much."

"Me neither."

"Just in case there's a happy ending, I'll grab the other bottle of stuff from my things."

He lays down on the bed and I find the lube at the bottom of my bag. I strip down to nothing and wince at the pain in my ribs. I'm going to need X to use some magic there too if he can. It's great my face doesn't look like it had a fight, but I'd like to move without wincing too. Especially with the man I'm currently sharing a bed with.

When I grab both bottles and turn around, I nearly scream when I see Dave's back.

"Are you almost done? I'm dying over here. I hope that lotion works well."

When I say nothing, he lifts his head my way.

"What's wrong?"

"I don't think lotion is going to help you," I whisper.

Dave rolls and bolts off the bed into the bathroom. He spins around to look backwards into the mirror.

"What the fuck is happening, Chuck?"

Dave's voice wavers and I finally break from my frozen place and join him in the bathroom.

In the mirror, his reddened and peeling skin shows the unmistakable outline of feathers.

"I think you're growing wings."

DAVE

Charles's fingertips dust over the new... addition on my back. Gentle and reverent is his touch, and it shouldn't comfort me so much, but it does.

"Does it hurt at all?"

I shake my head, still staring at the reflection in the mirror.

"It's just itchy. Can you... will you still put some lotion on and see if it takes away the itch?" I pause. He's still sore and recovering. I should be taking care of him. I'm just itchy, but he was some asshole's punching bag. "I mean, if you're ok to? You've had a traumatic experience. I want you to be okay first."

"The magic helped. My ribs are still sore, but I'm okay. Let me do this for you."

Swallowing, I touch my forehead to his. "If you change your mind after you start, please tell me."

"Of course I will. Go lay down again. It will be easier for me."

Returning to my position on the bed, I bury my face in the pillow while Charles positions himself over my ass, his warm ass cheeks against the small of my back.

"Is this okay? Are you comfortable?" he murmurs, and I nod because I don't trust my voice.

The snick of the cap on the lotion bottle precedes the sound of a squirt and his hands are on my back with a feather-light touch. The lotion is cool, and I shiver.

"Sorry, I should have warmed it for you."

"S'okay."

The gentleness of his hands as he works the lotion into my itching skin seeps into my resolve to remain calm. Every light stroke and touch across my back is a direct line to something in me I can't name, and I find the pillow wet.

Gentle lips on my neck draw a gasp from my lungs.

"I know it might not mean much, but you're the most beautiful man I've ever been with, Dave." He lays a gentle bite at the nape of my neck and continues to kiss my head, his nose in my hair. "I don't know how you're feeling with whatever is happening to you on the outside, but it doesn't change how I feel about you on the inside."

His words are like a balm to the bruised heart I've protected for years as I've floated through existence, wondering why I was so different. This feeling of finding someone who understands my pull between the world I was born to and the world I'm now in brings a rush of new, unexplained things inside my chest.

"Let me turn over."

Charles adjusts so I can turn onto my back, and I pull him down to straddle me. Needing him to be in the most intimate of contact.

He wipes the wetness off my face and kisses me with a kiss as soft as a butterfly's wing.

"Our existence is meant to change as we grow older. No one ever stays in the same line their whole life, Dave. As humans, we often grow and find new things about ourselves."

"I'm not human though, remember?"

"How can I forget? But I don't see a demon when I look at you. I never have."

Swallowing, I allow myself to drown in the depth of his green eyes when he firmly holds my head in place.

"Tell me what you see then, Chuck. Because I don't know what I am anymore. Demons don't grow feathered wings."

His smile is soft and sweet. "I see a man. A man who disregards his safety for others, who breaks rules he thinks aren't fair, and who is literally my biggest fantasy. I thought about you and there you were."

I can't help the smile that forms.

"Of all the times I've been able to see people's thoughts and actions, that one is my favourite."

"I liked those actions, too." He grinds his bare ass against my semi-hard cock and bites his lip. "I want it to be real. Not a dream. Right now, please."

"I don't want to hurt you, my love."

The endearment leaves my lips as naturally as a breath from my lungs. Charles remains still as his fingers curl into my chest. His gaze stays locked on mine and he grinds back again with a soft moan.

"You won't hurt me… love. Trust me, please?" He leans forward, burying his face in my neck and his hot breath across my ear is my last straw. I will do whatever this man ever asks me to. "You will always be the beautiful mess who entered my life when I needed someone to see me. It doesn't matter where you came from or what you are."

Sitting up, he reaches behind him to take my hard cock in hand. He snags the lube bottle on the bed and fills his hand with so much I have to laugh.

"No wonder you buy the economy size. That seems like a lot."

"Well, you get extra hot during sex. I figure I can't be too careful, and the more lube, the better."

"Extra hot?"

He slicks the puddle of lube over me and my eyes roll back.

"Yeah, it's like your body temperature skyrockets. It's… hot." He notches my cock at his entrance, his eyes locked on me with a desire I've never seen from anyone before. "I won't break, Dave. Fuck me like I begged you to the day I met you."

Growling, I flip him onto his back, pinning him to the mattress, and the wicked smile of the freaky priest I first met returns.

"You might beg me to stop, sweetheart."

"Nope." He pops the P and wiggles under me. "I want this. And you."

He whimpers as I press forward, waiting for him to relax and take more of me. When I finally slide home, my balls pressed against his ass, he's smirking at me.

"I wish you hadn't waited to do this, Dave." He flexes his hips upwards. "Do it."

Crazed with lust for being inside this man, this human, who has crept into every pore on my body, I give in. Pounding into him, the bed shaking and Charles grinning up at me with the satisfaction of a cat who got the mouse, I fucking lose my mind.

Splaying his legs out to the side, I own him. With every slap of flesh his loopy smile of satisfaction spurs me on. He raises his arms to push against the headboard and his eyes flick to my head.

"Your horns," he rasps, and reaches a hand up as I dip my head down towards him. His fingers trace the horn with the same reverence he did the first time and a shudder races down my back.

"Don't stop. I fucking love it when you do that."

One arm bracing himself and the other hand stroking my horn, I fuck him hard until he comes across his stomach with a low moan. Then I keep going until he's limp and sweating and his whole body trembles from overuse.

"I'm marking your insides. There's nobody else but me, Chuck. You hear me? Nobody else gets in this ass."

"Only you." His breathless exclamation flicks a switch, and I come with a feral roar, emptying into him.

Shaking, I lower myself over his body, not caring about

the mess we've both made and I try to catch my breath, but Charles isn't allowing it. He curls his fingers into my hair and pulls my head back.

"Thank you."

I kiss his lips. Maybe too hard, since he gasps again. "For what?"

"For trusting me and giving me what I asked for."

"I'll always give you what you want. Always."

Clearing my throat, I untangle us and roll off the bed.

"I'll get the bath started for you."

I can't look at him right now because the realization of what I just said is true has clawed into my skin. As long as Charles is in my life, there's nothing I won't do for him.

And that's awfully close to being in love.

I'm so grateful Chuck is a deep sleeper. I made more noise than a bull in a china shop searching for clothes to throw on in all the shopping bags. This time I won't show up in the kitchen shirtless and in pants three sizes too small.

Once in the kitchen, I search for a light but there's no need. X uses magic to flick it on for me.

From the sitting room next to the kitchen, he sits in the dark wrapped in a fuzzy bathrobe with what looks like a teacup in his hand.

"Do you ever sleep?" I ask as I reach for the covered plate of cookies on the counter.

"I could ask the same of you. At least you're wearing clothes this time."

"Touché."

Pouring a glass of milk and stacking four cookies on top, I join X, taking the seat across from him.

"I couldn't sleep. There's lots on my mind and I didn't want to wake Chuck. He's been through a lot. Oh! That reminds me. He was wondering if you could do one of your spells to help with the pain in his ribs."

"I absolutely can. How is he feeling?"

"Sore, but that's mostly my fault." I stuff a cookie in my mouth as X smirks.

"I bet. The walls are thin here, FYI."

Cursing under my breath, I shake my head. There doesn't seem to be many secrets in this house and I guess I'll have to get used to it.

"You know, Mike told us we were free to stay here and we should get to know each other. So if you don't mind me asking, is there a real reason you don't sleep or are you just naturally not a sleeper? I should know to be prepared all the time if you're lurking in the dark."

"Nightmares." His voice is so soft I have to strain to listen.

"I get them all the time and since I hate them, I just stay awake to avoid them."

"I'm sorry. I didn't mean to sound insensitive."

"It's okay. You didn't know."

"Do you want to talk about it?"

He cinches his bathrobe tighter and stares into his teacup. "Maybe another time I would. Thanks for the offer."

We sit together; me munching the cookies and X sipping his tea, and it's a comfortable silence. Like we could probably learn to be friends.

"When is your dad arriving? Should I have an offering or something when he gets here?"

"A what?"

"I've never met a demon before. Well, aside from you but I know you're different, so that doesn't count. I mean a real demon who might decide to incinerate me on the spot if he's angry. I just want to know if I should make his favourite cake or something?"

"What do you mean, I'm different?"

His eyes widen, perhaps regretting his choice of his words. But he doesn't know about my mother. So what else is there?

"Oh, ah, I'm sorry. I didn't mean to offend, but I'm a witch, right? Not a very good one, but that's what I am. Part of my magic is seeing what's under the mask. I sensed your horns when you walked in and... something else that's not quite clear."

"But you've never met a demon before. How would you

know I'm different?"

X sips his tea before placing it on the table and leaning forward.

"Your aura isn't filled with the evil of a demon like it should be. It's not as black. It's cloudy and hard to read but there's this... I don't know, like a shine to it. That's how I know you're different."

"And what about Charles? Is that how you knew he was the human?"

"Pretty much. His aura is the kaleidoscope most humans have, but when you arrived, there was a thread." He uses a finger to draw a line in the air. "There was a thread from his aura to yours that I'd not seen before."

"Is that bad?"

It takes X so long to answer I inhale a huge breath when he finally does.

"I don't think so. Auras connect you, not usually like that, but then again, most people can't see them either." He cocks his head as he watches me chew my last cookie. "Do you love him?"

If someone had asked me that question three days ago, it was an emphatic *no*. But so much has happened. So much has changed, not just between us, but with myself. Learning my mother was an angel, being sent here to be a better demon, meeting Charles in the most erotic way imaginable. Fuck, I've claimed him in front of others and I've threatened people who wanted to harm him.

I made him promise he's only mine.

"I've never known the feeling of love. My family was cordial to each other. Protective, but only when it was for their best interests. But this with Charles is different, and it scares me."

X's eyebrows pop up.

"It scares you? How?"

"I've seen what humans do to each other without reason or cause. They're a lot more mean than demons sometimes. Hurting another's heart is commonplace. There's often no real thought to the consequence of the other once one has got what they wanted. And it's a lot to take in along with the stuff about me and my mother. What if it's love, and he doesn't feel the same? Where does that leave us? We were supposed to have seven days together, and then I was to go back to where I came from."

"And now?"

Staring at the ceiling, I puff out a breath.

"Now eternity doesn't feel like enough time with him."

X leans back, soft smile in place.

"That, my new friend, is l-o-v-e. You should go tell him." He rises and picks up his teacup. "I'll put my headphones on. Knock yourself out with all the physical affection you need."

X leaves me alone and I take my glass back to the kitchen, pausing to stare out the kitchen window. The moon is bright again tonight and I wonder if it's romantic to tell your lover under the light of the moon you're in love?

Charles

When I roll over expecting to find the overheated body of Dave and it's only a cold spot on the bed, I blink open my eyes to look at the clock.

It's 2 AM, and the bed has been empty for a while. Movement outside the patio doors catches my eye. Without thinking of clothes, I walk over to investigate. I must admit, this whole naked wherever and whenever business is fantastic. I'll have to get back into being mindful once I leave here and find a place, but until then, I'm free to be... well, *free*. I can finally understand the hype over nudists.

Sliding the door open, my eyes widen to find Dave reclined on the lounger. His head turns at the sound of the door and he sends a sinful grin my way.

"I thought it was only me who liked to bathe naked in the moonlight."

Dave laughs softly. "I guess I'm discovering a lot of new things about myself, just like you." Patting the space between his legs in invitation, I crawl into the spot and lean back against his chest.

"Is that what kept you up?"

"Mostly. I couldn't turn off the thoughts."

His arms squeeze around me and even with the cool night air against our skin, I'm warm. "When I couldn't sleep as a child, I often prayed. My foster parents were very catholic. Prayer was their answer to everything."

"Did it help?"

My mind rolls back to the days I was a very confused teenager. I always focused on the prayers I liked best and not the ones I know they chose, hoping through prayer I'd discover I didn't like men. It was difficult to find my way for a long time.

"When I found a balance and prayed the way I wanted to, it did."

"Maybe you could teach me how one day?"

"Because you want help to sleep or for something else?"

He places a kiss on my temple. "Because I... I want to know more about you. And I need to adjust, I suppose. A way to cope with all this stuff. All these feelings."

I don't answer for a few moments because I know Dave is searching for words. His swallows are loud in the quiet of night, even with the random cicadas hum. I don't know what he wants to say, but I know what I hope he says.

"My father will be here tomorrow. Would you meet him with me?"

"Of course. I'll be there if you need support. Is he, I mean, will he be okay with me there? I'm not a priest anymore, but he might still get those vibes from me? I don't know if demons get vibes like that, though. I'm just saying I don't want him to be uncomfortable with such an important talk."

Dave's chest rumbles with laughter against my back and I reposition to straddle him instead.

"Why are you laughing at me?"

"You're nervous about meeting my dad."

"Well, he's some kind of high-ranking demon and I don't want to embarrass you. I mean, I propositioned you in the kitchen the first time we met. I don't want to be so bold with your dad."

"You plan on propositioning my father with me sitting there?"

"What? No! That's not what I meant at all! I meant, I just don't want to say something out of line. Like hey your son is amazing and please don't make him go back. I'll do whatever you want if he can stay."

I meant it as a joke, but once the words are in the air, I know it's true. I don't want Dave to go when his week is up, and I just might make a deal to have him a little longer. A future without Dave isn't that appealing.

"Is that what you think? I'm amazing?"

Leaning forward, I touch my forehead to his. "I don't want you to go."

Pressing a kiss to his lips, I squeeze my eyes shut and just say what I've been thinking. What's been on my mind since Mike's comment forced me to examine what's been happening in my heart.

"I think I love you and I know I might do something stupid if it meant I could keep you longer with me."

It should feel good to get that off my chest and let him know, but it hurts to breathe the longer he stays silent.

"Chuck..." He puffs out a shaky breath and I try to burrow into him farther. I can't look him in the eye if he can't say he's at least maybe sort of attached to me. I won't survive another romantic rejection.

He'll have none of me hiding though and he sits up, effortlessly taking me with him as he scoots to the edge of the lounger. I wrap my legs tighter around his waist and inhale the unique scent of Dave. The oatmeal lotion from earlier mixed with his masculine musk.

Placing his hands on the side of my head, he forces me to look at him.

"I asked him to come earlier because I don't want to go back."

"What?"

"I'm not a demon, Charles. I'll never be what I'm supposed to live up to. But I'm no angel either. I make mistakes and I often blur some lines of what's bad and good." His lips touch my forehead and my fingers curl into his shoulders. "The only place I can exist and be who I truly am is here. Where everyone has a bit of demon and angel in them, and I'm not held to some high expectation for either."

Dave's blue eyes fix on mine with a fierceness that will forever be seared in my mind.

"This is how you feel, isn't it? All the things you've been doing they taught you are shameful and wrong, and they aren't. And now that you're free from the pedestal the church put you on, it's like this giant yoke on your shoulders has lifted."

Nodding, I whisper, "Yes. That's exactly it. For the first time in my life, I've been able to be me... and I don't want to go back to my old life. I'm not afraid to say I find great joy in all the things considered so vile I was trained to wipe them from my thoughts. But I also don't know what to do going forward."

"I'll help you figure it out." Another kiss, this time deeper and longer, and I melt into him, knowing in my heart of hearts he would. We're not conventional. There's nothing normal about any of this. Yet, I can't imagine anything different now.

Dave groans into my mouth, and his cock thickens beneath me. I wiggle back and adjust on his lap so I can take us both in hand.

"Fuck..."

I smile against his neck, rubbing myself against him. Chasing that release we both want. It's not gentle or tender. It's raw and filled with a desperate passion I'll never get enough of. His mouth crushes mine as his hands roam everywhere at once, searching for a place to stay but never content to stop long.

"I'm gonna come." He mumbles against my lips, breathless and needy.

"Wait for me. I'm almost there." I gasp against him as he

tenses and it's a rush, but I cry out with my orgasm seconds before he does. His arms crush me to his chest.

I'm sated and hyper emotional. And my body cries out for proper sleep.

There's a flutter near my face, a delicate puff of air, and I open my eyes.

Gasping, I look up to find Dave, wide eyed at the enormous wings cradling me.

"Dave... are you okay?"

He nods slowly and shifts, making the feathers graze against my exposed skin, and I shiver. "I think so? It's just... I was about to tell you something and then they just popped out."

"What did you want to tell me?"

"That I love you too."

The morning comes far too quickly after our moonlight confessions. They filled me with so much hope for a new beginning, I woke refreshed. I was in love and Dave didn't want to leave. I didn't need coffee to perk me up.

Dave was another story.

He was irritable with the wings, trying to figure them out.

We spent some time learning how to control them. Just like his horns, they stayed hidden most of the time. While the horns showed up when he was horny or angry, the wings seemed to come out when he felt content and happy. We didn't know how it would work with clothes on, but I, for one, was more than happy to help figure it out.

It appears I have a thing for feathers and horns. Who knew I'd be so into such things? Certainly not me. I was just happy they came with a man I already knew was the perfect match for me.

But Dave is nervous this morning. And I can understand why.

He opted for his usual fitted suit, pleased that the wings tucked in and out of sight just fine. I was still dressed only in my boxers, unsure of what to wear and still half afraid his father would send him away and he'd be gone forever. A thought I couldn't bear to hang on to for long or I'd drown.

I thought of digging out the last joint I had left, just to create a chemical calm, but that didn't seem like a good idea meeting your lover's parent for the first time while high.

"You haven't changed your mind, have you?"

Dave's voice breaks through my thoughts, and I shake my head.

"No. I'll meet him, but I want you to have time alone with him first."

"What? Why?"

He stalks out of the bathroom over to me and takes my

hands in his.

"I need you there, Charles. I don't know if he'll understand everything I want to say, and you're the only one who gets it like I do."

"Just go ahead without me and I'll be there after. I think it's important for you to have some time alone. What if you never see him again?"Dave's brow furrows, and I touch my hand to his cheek.

"Please, let me give you some time alone. I promise I'll be there."

He brings his lips to mine, and with a sigh, I allow him to take what he wants. What he needs in order to get through what's ahead.

When he steps away, leaving me short of breath, his lopsided smile flips my gut upside down.

"You know where to find me."

Dave lets the door close behind him with a click. I count to ten to make sure he's actually moving down the hall before pulling a shirt on and stepping outside with my rosary. As much as I want to, I can't turn my back completely on my faith. Just because the church wasn't open and accepting doesn't mean I can't be.

Perching on the edge of the lounger, the smooth beads sliding through my fingers calm my racing thoughts. I initially thought I should pray for forgiveness, but I'd not done anything wrong. Well, the stolen money was wrong, but everything else wasn't. I could correct the money issues easily enough.

But the purpose I had before was missing. I had no life direction anymore, and I needed it. All this time I had been preparing to leave the church, I hadn't thought about what I'd actually do once I left. I'd been too caught up in all the worldly pleasures I wanted to pursue, and I didn't give serious thought to my future.

"Hey."

I smile as X stands a few feet away, his long hair not back in its usual bun. He fiddles with the rings on his left hand.

"Hi. Do you need to talk?"

I don't know him well enough yet, but he's not himself and since we all seem to be going through rough times here, it's only polite to offer an ear.

"I, uh, Dave said you asked if I could do magic on your ribs. Thought I'd pop by and see if it's a good time, it doesn't take long."

"Oh, yes! I'd love that."

He smiles and eases down next to me.

"What do you need me to do?"

"Just sit. But I have to touch you. Is that okay?"

"Of course it is. I assumed you would."

X has never been this jumpy. Hell, he made a pass at me out here before with no nerves.

"So, this is a touch healing. I'm actually good at it. You don't have to worry. It works better if I can touch your skin directly."

"Oh, yeah. I can do that." I pull my shirt off over my head

quickly and X averts his eyes.

"Is something wrong? If you don't mind me saying, you seem... jumpy. If you're worried about Dave getting all caveman with you, he won't. He's gone to see his dad, anyway."

X moves his hand over my rib cage, pressing his palms into my skin. It's warm and tingly.

"If I talk to you it's confidential, right? Like, I know you're not a priest anymore, but you'd keep it a secret?"

He continues to only look at where he's touching me and moves to another area. I watch a bruise fade right in front of me. It's the oddest thing.

"I think this rib is cracked. It might feel weird."

A zing goes through my side, not unpleasant but also not something I'd like to keep happening. I wiggle. "Sorry. You're right, that's weird."

"So I told you they kicked me out of my coven, right? Well, something happened the other day and I'm worried. I don't know what to do."

"What makes you worried?"

He says nothing for so long, I think he may have changed his mind about talking.

"I mix with humans a lot and I met someone I really like. If we were to... um, be intimate, I'd have to tell him I'm a witch." He shifts his hands again and I wonder how much practice he has with this because he's comfortable and confident. Not at all how he is with spells in the kitchen.

"And you don't want him to turn you away?"

He nods. No words and he lets his hair cover his face.

"There are rules to follow…" He stands, shoving his hands in his pockets. "You should be all good now. You better get going. Dave needs you."

X spins and retreats quickly, leaving me hanging, wondering how I can help. Grabbing my shirt, I enter our suite again, closing the patio door with one last glance to see if X came back to talk more.

But he's right. Dave needs me.

Dressing quickly, I leave our room to meet him and his father, and pray the outcome is what we both hope it will be.

Dave

My dad's message said he'd be here by 11 AM. He assured me he'd get here even though he wasn't certain of where it was.

The kitchen is empty, and my smile drops when I notice X isn't here to create some casual chatter to get my mind off the coming conversation. But I can tell he was here earlier.

A freshly baked coffee cake sits on the kitchen table, and that brings my smile back as I remember our conversation last night and X's demon offering. Like he had to gift Dad a goat or something. Coffee cake is a much better option.

A thud sounds from the hall closet, followed by a muffled curse, and I laugh at the entrance of my father as he bursts from the coat closet with a box of mittens in his hands.

"Hey, Dad. Underworld transportation sure likes their closet drop-offs, don't they?"

He growls down at the box of mittens in his hand like they've offended him and tosses it into the corner.

"They sure do, and it's a pain in the ass. We should have better entrances than that. I'm not here to sort mittens,

I'm here to deal for your soul. For fuck's sake, let me walk in the front door and if that can't happen, how about a shower instead? At least I'd be greeted with naked flesh for the improper entrance."

With my hands stuffed in my pockets, I rock on my heels and agree with him.

"I hear some people offer their soul for a decent pair of mittens though. Might be an opportunity there for you. It gets cold here."

Dad shudders. "I don't know how they stand the cold. I like my constant, pleasantly warm temperature."

Dad mimics my stance. "So, are you going to invite me in or are we going to stand here staring at each other while debating winter wear all day?"

"Oh, right. Um... come in."

Leading him into the kitchen, I motion for Dad to have a seat at the kitchen table. The rings on his fingers clink as he hitches up his dress pants before sitting. He leans back in the chair, resting one ankle on a knee. I smile when I see the patterned socks of tiny Yoda's I gave him for his birthday one year. *Yoda Best Dad*. I thought it was funny.

"Um, X, he lives here. He made the coffee cake this morning. I was hoping you could meet him, but he's not here."

Dad takes the napkin I hand him and pulls a piece of cake off the already sliced pile.

"He's not the one you're sleeping with, is he?"

Coughing on a bite of cake, I shake my head.

"Jeez, Dad. No. And why would you ask that?"

He shrugs with a small smile. "There are some things a father just knows."

"Mike told me about my mother." Dad's hands pause briefly as he brushes his crumbs into a pile. "Were you ever going to tell me?"

My father at least has the grace to look embarrassed.

"Truthfully, Dave, I was hoping I'd never have to."

"What? I don't understand."

Dad sighs and pulls the coffee cup towards him I set down earlier. He runs his finger along the edge for a few moments before he meets my gaze again.

"I know it doesn't seem like it, but I had a weakness when I was younger, and her name was Celestella. She was the most beautiful, funny, witty woman I'd ever met. I was under a spell whenever I was around her."

I've never seen such a wistful look on my dad's face before.

"How did you meet? Do I look like her at all?"

Dad's half-smile tugs at my heart.

"You have her eyes and her smile." Dad sips his coffee before relaxing back into the chair again. "I was to break up a newly formed church. The area was leaning too heavily into religion, and we were concerned the few demons on earth full-time would be hunted down. Ella, that's what I called her, was a parishioner there. She was so very passionate about the cause." He sighs again and I feel the weight of it to my bones.

"Was she... did she bargain for you?"

"Do I own her soul, you mean? No, nothing like that. She was too good for that. Even I knew she'd never give her soul to me. I was just a handsome ruffian sitting in the back, keeping tabs on things. I may have had a silver tongue for those of weaker character, but it never worked with Ella."

"Did she know what you were?"

Dad's face falls, and a genuine sadness appears. My dad has always been so confident and powerful. Heavy-handed even. But I've not seen that kind of sorrow on his face before today.

"She only found out after I revealed myself to her by accident. By then, it was too late. She was already pregnant with you."

His voice is so broken and sad. Like I'd feel if I had to leave Charles behind.

"When an angel and demon have a child, Dave, it's beautiful and tragic and we never know what the offspring will do in the world. When your mother knew she was pregnant, her only wish was for you to be loved and for me to give you a chance."

"How did she die? Did she ever get to meet me?"

She sounds like such a wonderful person. If she reduced my dad to a sentimental mess, she must have been amazing.

"When an angel gives birth to a child who carries traits of someone like myself, they... they give all of themselves to the child in the hope they'll be a better being. Good out weighs the bad sort of thing. Someone who will do the best for the world that they couldn't do." He swallows. "It's all or nothing when good and evil collide like this."

Exhaling a shaky breath, I let his words tumble around my brain until the real meaning of them finally hits me. And the ache in my chest is so tight a sob escapes my lips.

"So she died just to have me?"

"Yes, but she did it with so much joy and love, Dave. There was not a moment she wasn't happy knowing you would be born, even when it meant the end of her. She made me promise her, if you showed any signs of being more angelic than demonic, I was to encourage you to follow it."

"But I've been struggling my whole life trying to be what you want and you've not said anything until now. Why now?"

Dad looks away, more vulnerable than he's dared to show at home. If he wasn't wearing the socks I gave him, I'd think someone else was here in his place.

"I'm a demon, remember? I'm selfish and even though your mother was the only woman I ever loved, if I couldn't have her, I wanted you. You reminded me so much of her. You made it worthwhile to know I lost her."

What is taking Charles so long? He'd have something profound to say by now, and I'd not feel like I was being ripped in two.

"But you were breaking a promise doing so."

He nods.

"When you were eight and your brothers were burning ants under a microscope, you know what you did? You rescued worms from the lawn after a rain. You knew they were easy pickings for the birds and you'd rush around picking up as many as possible and hiding them under plants and burying them in soil." He sighs again. The heaviness of this conversation is palpable with every word and breath. "I knew then it was likely your mom would win, and you'd be an angel. But I didn't want to let you go. It wasn't enough time."

Dad's eyes are warm as he reaches over and lightly squeezes my hand.

"Do you know about... the physical stuff that's happening?"

He smirks, a return of the dad I'm used to showing once more.

"Is something happening?"

My cheeks flush, thinking of how to tell my dad about the wings. I don't know why, but it's like when I was a teenager and getting the sex talk.

"Uh, well, I have these now." Standing, I remove my coat and dress shirt quickly and right there in the kitchen in front of my dad, I spread my wings. Dad's eyes shimmer with unshed tears. "I, uh, my horns don't get as big when I'm... uh... when I'm aroused. And, um, these have been brewing for a few days. I was pretty itchy and last night they just sort of popped out."

Dad smiles, but it doesn't quite reach his eyes.

"I was told that could happen when your internal psyche knew which side of the path it wanted to follow. You needed time to work it out and when you do, the change kicks in. Usually mitigated by an event or... a person."

"It was both, I think. Do you want to meet him?"

My dad smiles and nods.

"I'd love to. Is it the priest you mentioned?"

"Yeah, he's going through his own stuff. Figuring out his own path, like you said. I don't understand what the pull is and what all this stuff is I keep feeling, but it didn't happen until him."

Dad stares off into the distance and says nothing for a few minutes.

"You're a wonderful man, Dave. Just because I didn't get my wish for you to be all demon doesn't mean I'm disappointed. But with this change, you'll have special circumstances to maneuver. Wings don't make you an angel. Those horns are still there too. Life will be challenging sometimes because you may not know who you are some days. But if you've found someone who accepts this and loves you, anyway? You've found the needle in the haystack and I want to meet the man who loves my boy."

I move towards the hall but Charles is already standing there and a new ache that's foreign to my body settles across my chest. But it's a softer one and I find I don't mind it so much. He steps up to my dad and extends a hand.

"It's a pleasure to meet you, sir. I'm Charles. The one who loves your son."

My dad takes his hand and even though it's an emotional moment, his jaw sets, and I know he's testing Charles.

"So, is it still Father Charles?"

He shakes his head as he steps back. "No, just Charles. That's not my place anymore."

"And do you know where your place is?"

Licking his lips he glances at me before stepping closer.

"Wherever Dave is. That's where I'll be."

Dad seems satisfied with the answer, but he stands to go and I'm not ready for him to leave yet.

"Wait, Dad. What happens now? I mean, obviously I failed the test and I think I lost the damn handbook, anyway. But... do I have to go back?"

My voice wavers, and Charles squeezes my hand.

Dad shakes his head slowly.

"You can't ever come back, son. I can't protect you there anymore. Especially now that you have wings. You'd be killed."

"Can he stay here, then? Like, be here. With me?"

Charles's cheeks turn pink with his blurt and he mumbles under his breath, "I told you I'd say something bold."

"He has to. It's the only place a being with both visible traits can stay."

"So I'll never get to see you again?"

Dad stuffs his hands in his pockets and looks to his shiny loafer covered feet.

"Occasionally. Mike still keeps in touch. He owes me for eternity, remember? It's not forever, son. It's just for now." He turns to walk to the closet and changes his mind, heading for the front door instead. "I think I'll avoid the mitten route for the way back."

Just like that, my dad is gone.

Turning to Charles, I find him still staring at the door.

"I thought he'd be taller."

I laugh as Charles turns back to me, smiling. "Yeah, I thought he'd be all broody and dark and like seven feet tall. But he's actually a down-to-earth guy." He snorts. "Well, not down to earth, but you know what I mean."

"I do. Come here."

He steps into my arms and my wings wrap around him in the cutest feather cocoon. He laughs when a stray feather brushes his cheek, and I kiss him until he gasps for air.

"Whoa! Dude! When did the wings happen?"

X breaks our moment when he enters the kitchen and I shoot an unimpressed glance his way.

"You're in the kitchen, Dave. Topless again, too. I'm allowed to comment."

Charles laughs as I pull the wings away. "He has a point, Dave."

"So, I missed your dad. Did he try a piece of cake?"

"He did. Where were you?"

X shrugs and flops into a chair, reaching for the remaining cake slices.

"Took a walk to get outside. Smelled the roses. That kind of stuff."

Charles looks at me, and without words I motion for him to keep X talking.

"I found a gorgeous garden in the back. Do you maintain that? The roses were gorgeous," Charles says as he pulls out a chair at the table.

"Sometimes I putter about out there. Today a lot of the raspberry canes were all trampled, and some roses were broken though."

I cough and slip my shirt on.

"I'm gonna take a walk. I'll catch you both later."

Neither of them really hears me, already deep into a conversation about raspberries and rose gardens and when I glance back to see X gesturing with his hands and Charles laughing along, I pause.

We're such an unlikely group. But we all seem to fit somehow. Charles and X talk and laugh easily. X and I share a tether of a painful past. He hasn't shared it all with us, but he will. Charles seems to know what we each need to hear. Perhaps that's from years of experience listening to people in a confessional.

Either way, I already can't imagine him not with me.

Charles turns his head to find me still standing in the doorway and he cocks his head in question. I tap the space over my heart and nod. He smiles back, holding my gaze a little longer than normal, and a filthy image flashes behind my eyes. I gulp a lungful of air and stare back at Charles.

He winks and turns back to X.

Chuckling to myself, I shake my head as I leave.

I said he could suck a dick like nobody's business. Good thing I'm nobody.

CHARLES

After speaking with X for what felt like forever, we finally say our goodbyes and I hurry to find Dave. I know I don't need to worry about him, but tell my head that. It's ingrained in me to worry about people I care about.

But I also need to share with him my news.

When I don't find him in our suite, I exit the patio door with a giant grin. I know where he'll be.

It's hard to walk and not run, but somehow I manage. When I arrive at the small garden area, my smile falters when Dave isn't where I thought he would be. Did I get it wrong?

"Keep going, Chuck. You're not wrong."

With a laugh, I walk past the row of shrubs into the wild raspberry patch, where I find Dave with a small cup picking raspberries. His giant fingers deftly pluck the tiny berries without so much as a squish. I'm not sure why I love that. His gentle touch on a piece of fruit.

"Were you afraid I didn't get your filthy mind message?"

Dave pops the last raspberry in his mouth and strides towards me. He changed his clothes after meeting with his dad. No longer in a suit, but he's absolutely breathtaking in a pair of black sweats that hang low on his hips and a red t-shirt stretched across his chest.

"Well, a little. But I'm glad it worked. I wasn't sure if you'd get it since I wasn't praying or anything."

"No? You weren't praying for me to allow you to suck my cock in the garden again?"

Damn it. "Well, when you say it like that, it sounds desperate."

"You're not? You had to stop yourself from running out here to find me."

Throwing my head back, I laugh. Oh boy, this guy.

"Do you think we can work on this whole mind reading or tuning into my channel stuff? I'm not sure if I like you knowing what I want all the time."

He places the cup of berries on the ground before pulling me to him.

"I can try, but remember, *you* started this one. I enjoy knowing you can't get enough of me. I want you to always be like this."

Dave brings his lips to mine, but he doesn't kiss me. They brush over mine as he whispers, "So don't keep me waiting. Get on your knees, Chuck." He takes my hand and presses it to his crotch. "You want this in your pretty mouth?"

"Fuck, yesss."

He steps back, hooking his thumbs into his waistband, and pulling his pants down so the elastic sits just under his balls.

What a fucking vision he is. He strokes his dick with a raised eyebrow and I get the hint, sinking to my knees in front of him.

A line of drool seeps out of the corner of my mouth. He notices and runs the tip of his cock through it, smearing it across my waiting lips.

"You're so insatiable. Cock starved is what you are."

"Stop teasing me." I swallow back the saliva that just won't stop.

Dave thrusts into my waiting mouth as soon as I open it again. I grip his thighs, hanging on as he takes what he wants. What I want. His fingers tangle in my hair as he tugs me off his cock and I moan with frustration.

"Do you want to swallow it this time?"

"Why are you even asking? Just do it. You know I love it."

Which I do. Dave can use me like I mean nothing, but it never feels like it. He can be rough and gentle at the same time, which is the headiest combination for me. The most perfect combination.

He shoves my mouth back down his length, and I gag. A murmured *sorry* as I catch my breath and he's back at it. Using my throat for his pleasure as I struggle to breathe. Saliva flows out of my mouth and drips off my chin. My eyes water every time the head of his cock rams past my tonsils and the fucked up thing is I don't want him to stop.

Dave's muscles tense under my palm and his breath stops. It's like he's suspended in this tiny place only he feels before he cums. My entire body vibrates, waiting for what's about to occur.

He roars. That's the only way to describe the sound that leaves his mouth. It's like a lion I saw at the zoo one time. I can swallow the first few spurts when they hit my tongue, but I can't keep up, and tap his leg before I drown in cum.

He immediately releases his hold on my head and jerks himself through the rest of his orgasm. Dave throws his head back, lost in his pleasure, and he's the most gorgeous creature I've ever seen. His horns shine bright in the late afternoon sun and his throat bobs as he struggles to catch his breath.

"Fuck, you're so hot like that," I rasp and he descends to his knees in front of me.

"Me? Look at you. Such a fucking mess. All for me." He wipes my chin with his thumb and pushes it past my lips. "You bring out the demon in me with your cum filled requests."

Sucking his thumb into my mouth, I watch his eyes darken as my tongue swirls around it. He pulls it out, this time bringing his lips to mine. Tasting himself on me, and my breath hitches as he pulls me closer.

"I knew I'd find you guys out here."

X's voice fills the air and with a soft whoosh, Dave's wings surround me, hiding me from X.

"You need to wear a bell," Dave growls.

"You two should have sex behind closed doors and stop showing off if you don't want people to see you."

"That's no fun," I offer, and Dave gives me a pinch. "Ow! What was that for?"

"I don't like people to see you naked. I indulge your desires to be outside, but I hope nobody watches."

Oh. Okay, maybe it is kind of fun then.

"Anyway, Mike is back, and he was asking if you two were around to talk. I told him you were likely getting busy in the garden. So, clean up and join us in the kitchen when you can."

He whistles as he returns to the house, and Dave keeps me in this cocoon for a few minutes longer.

"We'll finish this later." He kisses the top of my head and stands, offering me a hand up. "Are you okay? I was pretty rough."

"Just how I like it." I tug on his hand towards the house. "Lets get cleaned up quick. I have lots to tell you."

We rushed through a shared shower that got a little handsy. I'm not the only one insatiable, it seems. But after speaking with X and now that Mike is back, my excitement bubbles over and for once I'm not thinking about boning the demon-angel dude who literally swept in and saved me.

As Dave bends over to search for his other shoe, grumbling under his breath about needing to buy something other than dress shoes, the domesticity of the scene slams into me. His clothes sit in a pile or are still in shopping bags. Mine are in boxes stacked neatly in the corner except for the ones I've folded and left on a chair. The bathroom counter is all my various hair products and shave creams, colognes and toothpaste. Dave has a single blue toothbrush set off to the side.

I've never shared a bed or space with anyone long term before. Matthew could never leave his things or spend the night. But Dave seeps into this space with me. Separate, but also together in more ways than I could ever hope for.

A new start, with everything I've ever dreamed of, is right here.

"Are you ready?"

Dave grumbles and tosses a shoe aside.

"Yeah. I'm just going with socks. Who needs shoes inside, anyway? We need to go shopping again, though. I need real shoes."

"Of course. We can go after we chat with Mike."

He walks over to me and slides his hand down my arm. "This time you don't leave my sight, though."

Threading my fingers through his, I tug him to the door. "I won't."

When we reach the kitchen, Mike and X are waiting with... lemonade.

"Sorry to keep you waiting." Dave pulls out my chair before settling next to me and pouring each of us a glass.

"Did you make this, X? I love lemonade."

"I did! First time. I hope you like it."

He watches as I take a sip, and it's good. When I smile and nod my approval, he beams.

"Are you all getting along well, then?" Mike asks.

"We are. A lot happened since you told me about my mother. Looks like I'm staying here for a while. Or permanently, if I can. You said this was a place for those who don't know where they belong, right?"

Mike nods with a small smile. "You're more than welcome to stay here. In fact, I'll probably need your help in the future. What about you, Charles?"

I glance at X, and he nods with a happy smile.

"I was wondering, since like you said, it's a place for beings who don't quite belong, if I could… if I could help them settle?"

Mike leans forward. "How so?"

"I have a strength. It's listening and helping others make peace. X and I had a wonderful conversation, and he mentioned there's been other beings that have been here but never stayed. I wonder if maybe they needed someone to assure them it was okay? Provide them comfort free of judgment."

A quick look at Dave tells me he thinks it's a great idea. He doesn't have to say a word. His warm hand on my thigh and soft gaze is enough.

"There's not supposed to be any humans here." My shoulders slump, and Dave tries to say something, but Mike holds up his hand. "But I recently learned some humans can mix with paranormal beings with zero problems. You might meet them one day. Such a wonderful couple and good friends of mine. John is a great baker, you'd love him, X. I know they'd appreciate having you to talk to, Charles."

"So I can stay and it's like a job?"

Mike chuckles. "I forgot what it's like to be someone needing to work for money. It's a job, yes, but you'll find you don't need to be paid living here. Whatever you need will show up. Even money." He nods towards Dave. "You can thank Faustus for that part."

"Is he like a sugar daddy demon? That's hot." X laughs as Dave tries to punch him in the shoulder.

"We're settled then. You're both staying and if you're happy with your suite, that's perfect. X runs this place well without me, so I'll leave you to it. I'm going to rest and then I'll be gone for a while again. Questions?"

We all shake our heads and Mike leaves us together in the kitchen.

"I knew he'd like your idea, Charles. I think it's great. I could have used you months ago, but I'm happy you're here now."

"Me too. I'm quite overwhelmed with everything. It's been such a blur. I'm just happy you helped me realize I could still offer comfort to those who need it and not need the church to do so."

X nods and pats my shoulder.

"I'm going to make dinner. You two can talk about the rest."

He winks at me and excuses himself.

"What do we need to talk about, Chuck?"

Taking his hand, I pull him to the front door. "Let's take a walk. Slip on those boots by the door. We won't be gone that long."

Dave agrees, slipping his feet into the ankle high rubber boots. He looks ridiculous, but he doesn't care. He's already reaching for my hand again as we step outside.

The farm style house of Mike's is on a country road. It's quiet, but I noticed a small group of apple trees when we were out last time. We walk in silence until we get to the group of trees, and I hop over the collapsing fence to the orchard.

"You're adding trespassing to your list of sins now? Remember, I don't need to learn to do that anymore."

Laughing, I watch Dave in his cute borrowed yellow boots step over the same fence to follow me. "I think we'll be okay. I just wanted someplace without distractions. This looked like a nice place."

We settle under a tree next to each other and Dave waits for me to speak. That powerful gaze on me like I'm the only thing he sees right now, and I have his entire focus. Which is how I always feel when I'm with him.

"I'm sorry for not asking how you were with your dad's news first. How are you with that?"

Dave's smile is soft as he brushes the back of his hand over my cheek.

"Don't apologize. It was a great BJ." He kisses my hand and settles back against the base of the tree. "I'm shocked, but also not. Knowing my mother was an angel, a real honest to god angel explains so much for me, Chuck. It's comforting to have an explanation as to why I struggled so much with the demon way of life. But, it's confusing. Like, I don't know what I am now."

"You're Dave. That's all you need to know. Someone who has found a place to belong and hopefully finds peace with that. You're protective, smart, sexy and when you need to be, you can be scary as fuck. You care, but you're also a hard ass if needed. You give people a chance, even when they likely don't deserve it. My opinion might not mean much, but I think you're the perfect combination and *that's* what you are."

Dave sits forward, leaning his arms on his knees.

"I'm not perfect. I know that. Nobody is."

"True. But you just went through some massive changes. You have wings, Dave. Wings. And horns. And yet, that doesn't seem to have upset your balance. You took it all in stride. You were barely even angry with your dad."

He pulls a blade of grass from the ground next to him and wraps it around his finger with a sigh.

"I couldn't be mad at him. Not after he told me he wanted to keep me because I reminded him of my mother. Or how she died for me, hoping good would win and I'd be the angel she wanted. I mean, yeah, it was unexpected, but I had two parents who wanted me to be the best I could be. That's reason enough to not be angry at the way it all played out."

I inhale a sharp breath with his words. His insight is far more than I expected. It makes me examine myself a lot closer, too.

"You have such a wonderful outlook on it. I need to learn from you."

He shifts, turning those deep blue eyes on me, and they're like a magnet, his eyes. They just pull me in, and I know if I had to walk away from him, I couldn't.

"When I met you, I was unravelling, Dave. Just like when your favourite sweater gets a loose string and you try not to pull on it, but somehow it just keeps falling apart. I knew I was close to the deep end. Drugs and alcohol aren't the way to cope with problems, but I felt I had no other choice. My foster parents already pushed me out. I couldn't talk to anyone in the church for fear someone would leak my secret. I sure as heck couldn't find a private therapist or again, the church would know. They kept close tabs on me. I had to battle through it on my own."

Dave takes my hand. "You're stronger than you know. When humans first meet a demon, they rarely react like you do." He smiles, wickedly as he no doubt remembers our first encounter, before turning serious again, putting me at ease like no one else has.

"Thank you. I'd like to blame it on the booze, but I think even then, I knew you were sent for me, Dave. If it wasn't for you, I'm not sure what would've happened. You saved me twice already from other people and you saved me once from myself. I prayed for help before and assumed it wasn't coming." I pause, organizing everything in my brain from this bizarre ride I've been on. As fantastical as it all seems, it couldn't be more real. "But I think you were, no... you *are*, the answer."

"C'mere." Dave leans back again, pulling me into his lap. "I'm going to make mistakes. We'll fight, but we'll make up. But one thing I know is I'd not be where I am now without you. Do you know why?"

I shake my head. "Why?"

"Because wings only show up when the heart finds its place." He cups my jaw and leans up to kiss me. "You're my place."

I don't know how long we sit under the tree kissing as lovers do. Slow and deep, with no care in the world. But it's the most peace I've felt in my mind for months.

The bark of a dog nearby snaps us out of our haze and we begin the walk back to the house.

Hand in hand, we follow the unpaved road, and I notice the rain clouds moving in.

"You didn't tell me your news." Dave smiles over at me and I laugh.

"Heh, I guess not. But you heard most of it in the kitchen when I asked Mike if I could stay here to help. I know I still need to be a listener or a helper to be happy. Not in a religious capacity, but just as someone who genuinely cares about other people. After speaking with X, he told me about some of the... beings that he's met at the house. It's a start of what I hope will make the rest of my life fulfilling. I need to have some purpose and this will do that. I hope."

The first giant raindrop hits my forehead. Dave gets hit too. We speed up our steps, but it's no use. The rain bursts out of the clouds, soaking us in seconds. My t-shirt clings to me and I pause in the rain to take it off.

"Oh, no. No, you don't." Dave shakes his head before bending and throwing me over his shoulder. "You're not getting naked out here, Chuck, for fuck sakes, save it for the patio."

He jogs us through the rain and I bounce on his shoulder, laughing as the rain falls and there's never been a time I've ever felt so complete.

EPILOGUE

6 months later

Dave

Sliding the patio open while juggling the glasses in my hand is no small feat. Especially when my beloved is naked outside. Again.

"Hey, babe."

Charles smiles sweetly at me as I set the gin and tonic sprinkled with fresh raspberries next to him. I wish I could say I've gotten better with him wanting to feel the air on his nakedness, but I haven't.

"Aww, you remembered the raspberries. Thank you."

Leaning down, I kiss his forehead before taking the seat next to him. When Charles didn't want to give up his newfound appreciation for being naked outside, I insisted we compromise. I gathered X and the two of us built a privacy fence around the small patch outside the patio door to our suite.

I didn't want to suppress anything he found he liked. He'd done enough of that, and I wanted him to know I loved him for what he was. Even when it brought a wave of possessiveness through me and out right jealousy if anyone else were to see him, I wanted him to be comfortable. Besides, it still benefitted me because I almost always felt the urge to mark him and claim him, even if the privacy wall was there. You can't find fault in a possessive fuck. We both win.

Charles sips his drink, humming his appreciation, and I lean back in my chair.

"Did you have an okay time talking to the new guy Mike brought by?"

Mike has shown a few to the house since we've been here. Growing up as a demon, I met all kinds of strange creatures from other worlds. It was never something that seemed different. I had to hand it to Charles, though; he was taking it all in stride.

"The vampire guy? Yeah, he's actually really nice. I don't know if he'll stay, though. But we had a great discussion. I hope it works out for him."

Charles stares up at the moon. Most people like to bathe in the sun, but with Charles, it's the moon. Again, I'm grateful, because his pale skin glows in the darkness and he's even more beautiful.

"I talked to my dad today."

He turns his head, all focus on me now.

"What did he say?"

"He said he could come for dinner and stay for a few hours."

"That's great! Are you happy about that?"

Not having had much time with my dad when I learned about my mother, it had been nagging at me. I wanted to know all about her. Charles convinced me to just ask my dad to come visit.

"I am. I'm looking forward to it. You'll be there, right?"

"Of course I will."

The silence is comfortable as we sip our drinks and I try not to get distracted over his naked body. Just once I should be able to come out here and not fuck him, but I'm a simple creature and it's hard.

Literally.

"Um, so, I went to the outreach center in town today."

Sitting up, I set my glass quickly on the table.

"And? How did it go?"

He puffs out a breath and turns to me.

"Good. I can volunteer there once I get a police background check. So I'll do that as often as needed. You're okay with that?"

"Why wouldn't I be? You want to help other young people from struggling like you did. It's wonderful, just like you."

"I also ran into a priest from my old diocese." Charles waits for my reaction and I promised I wouldn't overreact when he said it was a possibility.

"And by run into, do you mean with your car?"

His laugh fills the air.

"No. But he was polite and said he was sorry I left."

"Well, sorry doesn't cut it," I grumble, and Charles climbs

into my lap, forcing me to unclench my fists.

"It's enough. I'm not holding a grudge. Time is too precious. But I may see him there more, and I need to know you won't storm in and take me away over your shoulder."

He holds my face forward, forcing me to look into his green eyes.

"I promised I'd do whatever you need to be happy, Charles. I'd never do that to you. I might want to, but I won't."

"Thank you." He kisses me softly and wiggles on my lap. His bare ass brushing against my hard on. "But feel free to do it now if you like."

"Don't ever change your love for cock, Chuck."

I laugh as he grinds down on me harder.

"I only love yours."

"Good to know you only love me for my parts."

"Not true! But what am I thinking right now?"

He stares at me, brows knitted together, and my eyes just about pop out of my head when his message smacks into my brain. I stand quickly with him in my arms and almost walk smack into the closed patio doors.

"I knew you'd like that." He laughs into my neck and I'm so eager to get him inside I can't open the door until the second try.

I came to earth as a demon struggling to follow the rules and to fit into the only world I knew. When I met Charles, I never imagined he'd be the one to show me I fit perfectly in his world, just as I am.

"Have I told you I love you today?"

He laughs again as I finally get us through the door.

"No, but say it again with that thing you do with your tongue in my ass."

"Jesus, Chuck."

He slides down my body, and with a quick kiss; he leaves me there, staring after his bare ass as he walks to the bathroom, giggling the whole way.

Earth was to be a punishment, but it turned out to be the sweetest reward instead. He was not a missing piece, but an addition. Someone who enriched my entire life. I could be strong on my own, but together we could do so much more.

Spending forever on earth never looked so good.

Thank you for reading!
X's story is next!
My Dirty Witch

Acknowledgements

Thank you so much for reading! I had so much fun writing these two and I'm thrilled they finally made it to their own story.

I need to thank Dani for their thorough feedback and help with this book. You are a wizard with the tricky sentences I just can't seem to get right.

The people who beta read and added their input were no less helpful. Kota, Janice and Sarah, thank you so much for your help to get this book into the world.

Jenn! Thank you so much for making my words shine. Here's to many more projects together. Your genuine excitement really does urge me forward.

And to you dear reader, thank you! Paranormal isn't my usual thing, but this story just wouldn't be quiet and now I find myself with a few more lined up in the same little world of misfits.

This book was originally part of the Possessive Love Collaboration. Nothing has changed content wise, only the cover.

X's story is next and somewhere in my lineup will be Faustus, Dave's dad.

Until next time.

Much love,

RM

ALSO BY